My Boys

A Reverse Harem Romance

- Book 1 in the <u>My Boys</u> Duet -

By Alyssa Clark

Published by
Scarlet Lantern Publishing

SCARLET LANTERN
Publishing

Prologue

The First Meeting

The back tire hit a pile of gravel just as I started to follow the curve of the cul-de-sac, and the bike slid out from under me so fast, I didn't even get a chance to spin the pedals. I went down and heard the crack of the plastic and aluminum on the asphalt. Somehow, I managed to turn to catch myself on one knee and the palm of my hand. It burned, and a noise ripped out of me. I felt the tears in my eyes.

Don't cry, don't cry, don't cry.

A lump formed in my throat, and I tried to get untangled from my bike without making things hurt more. I hissed until I could turn over to sit on my butt. My hand smarted hard, and I could see the ripped-up skin while blood beaded up, making it burn even more. It made it harder to not let the tears drop. I took the time to inspect my knee. The leg of my coveralls was ripped, and I could already hear Mama fussing at how I ruined more clothes than she could afford to buy.

She wouldn't let me play outside again for the rest of the week, and I would probably get stuck helping her unpack. I didn't want to do that, which was why I was on the bike that Daddy bought me before we moved. The only problem was that the bike was too big for me, and I didn't know how to lower the seat. But I figured since I could reach the pedals with my toes, it was okay.

I was wrong, and the bloody mess of my knee was proof enough. I couldn't hold the tears back anymore, but I did manage to keep it to a sniffle as I hugged my knee.

I didn't notice the approaching sound of tires on asphalt, but when I heard a whistle, I tried to suck it all up. I tried to be tougher than I was. Three boys were across the big oval part of the cul–de-sac. A chubby brown-haired boy edged forward. There was a sprinkle of freckles across his cheeks, and his brown eyes were huge as he took in my bike.

"Nice." I could see the jealousy on his face when he said it.

"Touch my bike, and I'll kick all your asses," I barked, trying to puff up like I was bigger. I made an effort to keep the squeak out of my voice, hoping they'd take it as if I were just another one of them. I didn't want them to think I was just some stupid girl who didn't have a clue. I had my hair in a ponytail, but I knew that sometimes boys had long hair, too. That couldn't be a complete giveaway.

The boy who commented on my bike oh'd, probably at the curse word I used. I could already see he was a snitch, and if there'd been a parent around, he'd probably run to tell on me. The one in the middle, skinny with blue eyes and a shaved head, just nodded his head towards me. "You okay?"

I sniffed, the question seemed to make my hand and knee hurt more. "I ain't hurt," I shot back.

"Why does it look like you're about to cry?" the third boy asked. He didn't look like he was making fun of me. His skin was darker than the other two, and his hair was short and black. He just tilted his head as he looked at me. "Didja fall?"

"The wheel caught the gravel." I rubbed my nose across my sleeve, leaving a trail of snot Mama would fuss about. I just tacked another thing onto the list of why I was gonna be in trouble. "I ain't gonna cry."

The boy in the middle got off his bike and dropped it in the middle of the street. He circled my bike and crouched beside me, eyeing the rip in my jean coveralls. "You're bleeding," he stated the obvious. "C' mon, Bryce lives right there." He nodded towards the house we were in front of. "Mrs. Wilks can patch you up." He didn't wait for me to say anything; he shoved his hands under my armpits and tugged me up to my feet.

I fought a little, putting my weight down on the foot with the scraped knee. It hurt to the point I thought I was gonna fall. I grunted in pain, and the boy holding me tugged one of my arms across his shoulders. "Get our bikes out of the street," he said to the other two boys.

"Kay," was the response to the command, and the two boys followed us so they could drop their bikes in the yard of the house I was being led to.

"I'll get her bike," the chunky boy said, and I felt my blood boil.

I wanted to wail out another threat, but I didn't want my bike run over. So I just settled for giving him the stink eye. He acted like he didn't even see me, running his grubby hands all along the bright, shiny paint.

"That's Bryce Wilks and Noah Kemp." The boy who held onto me spoke lightly as we got to the door. "Bryce's mom, Mrs. Wilks, is like a second mom. She's

good about giving any extra attention if you need some."
He paused to knock on the door. "She's good about
listening to you when you gotta problem, too. If you can't
tell your own mom, if you know what I mean. She kinda
spoils Bryce, though, so he can act kinda bratty."

I figured Bryce was the chunky boy, but I bit the
inside of my cheek to keep from asking. Mama said no one
liked being called fat, and if I didn't want people saying
mean things to me, I shouldn't say mean things to begin
with.

"What about Noah?"

I got a grin. "He's my best friend. He's the best.
You'll see."

The door opened, and a lady with a brown ponytail
and a round face looked out at us. She looked a lot like
Bryce, and she took us both in with a surprised look.
"Lucas. Everything okay?"

"Found her in the street." He nodded his head
towards me. "She fell down and scraped her knee."

Her big, brown eyes turned to me, and I couldn't
keep from sniffling. She was a mom; she had that
superpower that pulled things out of kids. I could feel the
tears falling down my cheeks, and any hopes I had of
appearing like I was tough were crushed under the
shuddering feeling in my chest.

"Oh dear," she said and ushered us in. "C' mon,
hunny, let's get you cleaned up." This lady was magic, I
could tell already.

She directed Lucas to the bathroom right off the
living room, which was huge compared to the house Mama
and I moved into. There was a big couch that took up most

of the room and a television that looked like it had all the games. If this was Bryce's house, I could see why the other two boys hung out with him. He had all the cool toys.

I should've asked Daddy for a video game.

"Okay, sweetie, up here." With a little help from Mrs. Wilks, Lucas had me up on the countertop next to the sink, so she could get to work. She looked at my hand with a wince and carefully put it under the cold water from the faucet. "Did you just move in down the street?" She gave me a look before she pulled out the peroxide. "I saw the moving truck this morning."

"Yes'am." I tried to bite my lip to keep from whining as she cleaned up the scrapes.

"Where'd you live before?" Lucas asked, standing beside me. He gave my free hand a squeeze like he knew how bad it hurt.

I clenched my fingers around his. "The city." I didn't know how to elaborate on it. I didn't want to talk about the apartment we'd lived in. The only good thing I could say about it was the park when Daddy would take me to it.

"What's your name, sweetie?" Bryce's mom put a cool washcloth in the palm of my hand to staunch the sting from the peroxide. From there, she eyed the hole in the coveralls leg, looking at my knee.

"Francine." I pulled a face as I said it. I hated my name. It was terrible, and I was sure Mama gave it to me because she knew I wouldn't like it.

Magic mom powers saw just how I felt, and she hummed, "Don't like Francine, huh? How about we call you Fran or Frannie?" She carefully tugged the hole in the denim wider so she could dab at the torn skin of my knee with the burning disinfectant.

"It's an old lady name." I could hear the whine in my voice bounce back at me from the tiny bathroom. "I don't wanna old lady name." I twitched and tried to not pull away as she cleaned my knee. I clung to Lucas' hand hard, grateful that he hadn't just left me there to go play with his friends.

"My grandpa's name was Francis," he offered up as he looked at me with a seriousness I couldn't figure out. "Everyone called him Frank. We could call you Frank," he said like it made sense, like it didn't matter that Frank was a boy's name.

"Or Frankie," Mrs. Wilks amended. She carefully put a band aid on my knee and found one for my palm. "In case you decide you want to be a little girly."

"I like Frank." I nodded because I bet the boys wouldn't treat me like a girl while they called me Frank.

"Oh dear." The lady stepped back. "What I wouldn't give for a little girl. Then when we get one on the street, she turns into one of the boys." She released a sigh before looking at me. "All right, Frankie, you're all patched up."

"Thanks." I already felt better. There was just a little bit of a sting in my hand, and my knee didn't feel like it was gonna fall out from under me when I hopped off the countertop.

"Thank you, Mrs. Wilks," Lucas echoed beside me. He still held my hand. "We're gonna go play."

He led me through the house and back out the front door. I was tugged in front of his two friends, and with a surety I didn't have, he presented me to them. "This is Frank. She's one of us now."

1

Present Day

When I got into the bar, I could already see Lucas hunched over the bar top. His hair had grown to the point where it was a shaggy blond and was darker than the peach fuzz on his face. He looked at his phone, and when mine vibrated in my pocket, I knew he was adding to the group chat dedicated to the four of us. There were a series of replies that set off an echoing vibration. *I should turn the sound back on.* I didn't bother to pull out my phone to add to whatever our fearless leader was concerned with.

Lucas was the leader of our little group of friends, but he didn't direct us like a ruler. He was more like a concerned parent. I think it stemmed a lot from his dad not being in the picture, something I understood completely. After my parents split up, my dad took being a part-time parent to an extreme. It created some issues for me, and I could only guess what kind of issues Lucas still harbored towards his dad.

"What's up, Buttercup?" I singsonged as I climbed onto the stool next to him. I fished my phone out of my pocket and set it onto the bar top, spying bits of our group conversation as it flitted across the locked screen. "How long you been here?"

His face lit up, and he set his phone down before he leaned closer to me. "Half an hour at most." He shrugged his broad shoulders. "I knew you'd be late. I just figured Noah and Bryce would get here quicker."

"B is probably chasing tail." I didn't resist the urge to roll my eyes. "Man's gotta whore. Noah," I hummed, then thumbed open my phone, and navigated to the conversation. His last message said he was on his way, while Bryce's said he'd be another hour. "Noah's been working a lot."

"He's a junior attorney." I got a shrug for my troubles, like it would explain it all away. "He wants to make an impression, so he's gotta bust ass. Let the man do what he's gotta do."

"Gotta make Mama Kemp and Mama Wilks proud." I grinned before waving down the bartender for a beer. "Seriously gotta bust a lot of ass to satisfy all the neighborhood moms. You just have Mama Kemp and Mama Wilks to please." I winced as I considered the last time the two of us had talked. She'd taken me through the wringer because I'd talked about ending the relationship I'd been in. Kenny Barns was a med student who thought that since he was about to be a doctor, it was an excuse to be an asshole. I'd finally given up on the prospect of reality catching up with him. "My mom is way too critical for my liking. I'd take the disapproving looks of Mrs. Kemp all day any day."

"Mrs. Kemp's disapproving looks are always enough to set you on the right track," he assured me before tapping the brown bottle he'd been drinking from against mine. "Trust me, she was practically my second mom. All it'd take would be a hard look from her on a good day to get me to act right. Catch her on a bad day…" He whistled as a finisher to his statement. He gave me a look, eyeing me up and down, "Where's your man? I thought this was considered a 'group function' that he insisted he needed to be a part of?"

***

I snorted and didn't bother to refrain from giving my full attention to my phone. I typed a quick notification that I was there with a little snark, 'If you want attention, you'll get your ass here.' When I looked up at Lucas, he was looking at my phone too.

He snorted before he leaned his shoulder against mine. "Where is your man?" he asked again, like he knew my answer.

I took a deep breath. "Can't wait for the rest of the guys to get here before I air out my dirty laundry?"

"That bad?" He raised an eyebrow, pausing only to nurse on his beer. "I thought you said you liked him. What happened to that?"

"He started getting jealous." I heaved a sigh and relaxed against his shoulder. Lucas was a comfort. He had a quiet confidence that seemed to see every angle when I talked to him. If I was wrong, he wasn't afraid to tell me. He didn't kiss ass, and he didn't put up with my bullshit. He just listened to me. "Kenny objected every time we hung out. He didn't understand that we were just friends."

He nodded as he listened. "You have to understand, though…" He paused to sip his beer. "Dude was seeing you with three men. When you want something bad enough, sometimes you see all the things that'll take it away from you. Instead of friends, we were competition. He didn't see the fact that we're so close because we grew up together." He rolled the shoulder that was pressed against mine, bumping me off him and giving me a grin to soothe any offense it might cause. "The only people who are gonna understand what we are, are the people in our group."

I nodded, considering one of the accusations Kenny had made. "Do I have you guys in the friend zone?" I looked at him with a knot in my stomach, because I didn't know. There were times where it seemed like there was something more than platonic between us, but they were never blatant or obvious. Just having it called out at me with a face full of hurt feelings made me wonder if it were true.

Lucas laughed a little, looking away to flag down the bartender for another beer. "If any of us wanted something more from you, don't you think Bryce would've made a bigger effort to hold your hair back during your twenty-first birthday?"

"It's hard to hold a girl's hair when you're busy gagging," Noah said, magically appearing behind me and surprising both of us. His grin was infectious; it lit up his brown eyes and put emphasis on the dimple in his cheek. That dimple easily caught him a dozen girls. Coupled with him in a heather-grey suit, Noah was an irresistible force. He shifted on to the stool next to me and leaned in close enough to press a kiss against my cheek. "You were so trashed that night," he chortled as he pulled back. "And Bryce has a weak stomach. You're lucky he didn't upchuck on you while you were hugging the toilet."

"It's kind of the drawback with being friends with guys," Lucas admitted. "We can't handle it when you start throwing up." He looked a little green just from the conversation, and he set the bottle he'd been nursing aside.

"Besides, if any of us had been interested in that way, don't you think this conversation would've come up sooner?"

"What?" Noah looked curious, letting me know he'd only appeared at the last bit of what had been said. "So, this isn't just about Bryce's weak stomach? Here I thought we were getting ready to roast him. His birthday *is* coming up, and I'm all for that angle."

I turned to him. I wouldn't call Lucas a liar, but he would make excuses to spare my feelings. "Actually, I asked him if I had friend zoned you guys. Kenny said I had, and the three of you were just waiting for me to wise up." I tilted my head as I took in the other man I'd grown up with, and I took my time to appreciate the picture of him. Since Noah had begun the pursuit of his legal career, he had taken up a more put-together appearance that was a far cry from the torn jeans and muddy t-shirts he favored as a kid. "Do I have you guys in the friend zone?"

"Well, don't ask Bryce," Noah began with a grin. "Every girl who's ever told him no either friend zoned him or was a bitch. Because you know, he's a great package." He shrugged his shoulders, then continued, "Girl, I've seen you at your worst, and I know for damn sure you've seen me at mine. You know all my faults." He paused as if he suddenly seemed to consider something, then looked past me at Lucas, his tone of voice changing a little. "And I know yours. If we pushed for something more, what're the chances we could stay friends afterward."

"Priorities," Lucas spoke up from behind me. "Sometimes you have to think about what's more important and go with that."

"Oh." I nodded, then shot a smirk over my shoulder at Lucas. "So, I'm the one in the friend zone?"

Noah snorted and turned his attention to the bar with his hand in the air. "Priorities, Frankie. What's more important? Being my friend or getting in my pants? Because we all know you want a piece of this." He wiggled his eyebrows at me with that grin that I'd seen him give a dozen other girls.

"Okay." I turned back to Lucas. "I'm not in the friend zone then. This was good. Productive. Now, I just gotta find a guy that's not threatened by you dorks." I picked up my phone and shoved it back into my pocket. "At least," I settled in as I began a new thought that I knew would aggravate both of them, "you don't have to worry about me going through your friends."

"You'd only do that if you were desperate." Noah got a beer for himself, and his tone was jovial as he gave Lucas a look. "I mean, have you seen my friends? Clearly, I'm the hot one here." He took his time to adjust the lapels of his suit. "Neither of them can rock a look like I can."

"Yeah, but remember that the next time something breaks around the house. I'll be sure to charge you double when you give me a call," Lucas didn't look offended. Out of the four of us, Lucas was the hard worker. Something his mother influenced, though while we'd been growing up, I didn't see a lot of his mom. I met her in passing as she went from one job to another. Mrs. Kemp and Mrs. Wilks did the majority of looking after him. Then, as soon as he could work, he did.

That meant he wasn't around as much, and he didn't go to college with the three of us. I'd missed him, and I took moments like this to enjoy the company of my childhood partners in crime as much as I could. Maybe that was why Kenny thought there was more going on here.

"To priorities." I raised my bottle to them.

The people at the bar with me knocked their bottles against mine and echoed the sentiment. I felt like I was losing something there, but I wasn't about to admit that to either of the men beside me. Even if they were two of my confidants, this was something I was better off swallowing myself instead of stirring up trouble.

Because that's all that could do. Stir up trouble.

We were at the bar for nearly an hour before Bryce finally decided to grace us with his presence. While childhood had left him soft, growing up did him good. He towered over me like a wall of muscle that only dedication to sports could do. High school football helped burn away the baby fat but didn't help the entitled attitude in the least.

Bratty or not, I still loved him.

"Frankie!" he bellowed over the crowd before he barreled into me. A girl not much younger than me stood behind him. She wore a surprised expression that turned instantly into jealousy. It probably didn't help when he kissed my cheek and mauled me with a bear hug. "You've been MIA too long," he growled in my ear.

"I've been here for an hour," I protested.

"Yeah, but you missed last week." He pulled back with a pout and sniffed like he was offended. "Choosing other men over us. It hurts how you ignore our love," he continued like he hadn't brought a girl with him.

I rolled my eyes exaggeratedly, glancing behind the wall that was my friend to give his guest a look. "He's being an ass. Ignore him," I advised before tugging out the tangle of limbs that was Bryce.

"I gotta nice ass," he said, like he agreed with me. "Let's get a table instead of hanging out at the bar." He turned to the girl that had come with him. "Get me a beer and whatever you want." He had his wallet out and gave her a couple of twenties. "Shots if you want 'em." He turned, then went to the first high table he could find. "C'mon, bitches, we gotta catch up."

I almost felt bad, but I just gave his friend an apologetic smile before I followed him to the table. Noah and Lucas weren't far behind me, and I could hear the exchange between them. "This is why he goes through girls the way he does. They get sick of his shit and drop him when they're done taking his money," Noah observed. "I mean... I'd do the same thing if my dad was as loose with money as his is."

"You're making bank," Lucas snorted. "If your dad gives you money for anything, he expects to be paid back. I don't know how or why Bryce's parents still give him money. Didn't he get a full ride? Shouldn't you," Lucas directed his next question at Bryce, "have a job like the rest of us schmucks?"

"I have a job," Bryce scoffed as he tugged a chair out for me. I took it, then turned to receive a dark look from the girl with him. He threw his arm around my shoulders and only gave her a glance when she set his beer in front of him. "Physical therapy. I figure when this one finishes up residency and gets to be a full-fledged doctor, we can start a practice, and I can roll in some serious money."

"I'm not trying to be that kind of doctor," I protested and shrugged his arm off my shoulders. "Who did you bring with you? Quit being rude and introduce us." I hoped mentioning that he was being an ass would put me further in the girl's good graces. She wasn't the first B brought to us, and this was generally how he acted. Sometimes they let themselves be ignored while he bought them drinks. Sometimes, the girls would be assertive.

Being surrounded by a few good-looking guys could put women off-kilter, especially with someone like me in the mix. With the way I got doted on by the boys, it had to make them wonder what was up. I tried to put some distance between Bryce and me so I wouldn't step on her toes any more than he'd already insinuated. Hopefully, this would soothe her nerves.

I got what I thought was a grateful look before she flashed a flirty smile at the rest of my boys. She especially eyed Noah hard. "I'm Melissa."

Whelp, I misjudged.

A noise from across the table got my attention, and I could see Lucas must've come to the same conclusion. This girl was a good time and not long haul, I.E. Bryce's type. I released a sigh and leaned onto the table while Melissa chatted up Noah. He gave me a look while he entertained it.

"Priorities seem to be different for everyone," I pointed out to Lucas.

"It takes time to figure out what's important." He gave me a smile that didn't quite reach his eyes. I put all my focus on him, trying to figure out why. "When you know

what you want and what's important, which are you more
likely to go after?"

"What if what you want is what's important?" I
shot back.

His mouth opened like he had a retort ready, then
he paused, looking confused.

"Let's get shots!" Bryce interrupted the
conversation to send Melissa to the bar with the order.

"Your lady friend is not our waitress." I knocked
my fist against his shoulder.

"She wanted a good time and made me wait."
Bryce's lip curled while he spoke, his attention on Melissa
as she made her way back to us. "If she was more than just
a good time, then I'd be nicer. I'm not going for more than
what it is." He looked at me as he continued, "She knows
this and still wanted this." He gestured to himself like he
was a prized package.

I rolled my eyes. Despite all his posturing about
growing out of the baby fat, I still saw the chubby, freckled
cheeks. "There's nothing about that that's healthy, and
you're just making it worse for her. Quit being an asshole,
even if all this is for sex." I wanted to hit him or pinch his
arm like Mama would do to me while we were in church.
But I refrained because I got an odd look for Melissa.

"Don't like it?" Bryce sniffed at me before taking a
long pull at his beer. "Then make me stop."

Melissa and Bryce didn't stick around much longer
after that. There were two rounds of shots had before she
pulled him away from the table and towards the door. Then
Noah begged off, kissing my cheek a little sloppily. "I have
got a lotta work tomorrow." He had his arm around my

shoulders. "We need to do this more than once a week."
He threw in a little bit of a whine in his voice as he pressed
his forehead against my temple. "I miss you."

"Like you lost my number," I snorted.

"Priorities!" Lucas slurred from across the table.

"You're about to start residency," he puffed against
my cheek. "Not gonna have time to be one of the boys
anymore."

"We made it through with you getting buried in
studying for the bar exam." I hugged him tightly. "You can
put up with me working my ass off, too."

His phone chirped in his hand, and he sighed as he
let me go. "Call me when you get in trouble. The firm
doesn't handle malpractice, but I'll make sure we make
exceptions for you." He plucked up the suit jacket and
managed to look like he wasn't completely sloshed while
he walked out of the bar.

That left me with Lucas, something that happened
often enough. It was pushing midnight, and I had to report
to orientation at Mercy in the morning at eight. I just wasn't
willing to call it a night in favor of spending time with my
best friend.

"I wouldn't be here if it weren't for you guys." The
thought was drawn out of me, thanks to the depressant
qualities of alcohol.

"Think your dad would protest, seeing how he's
paid for the last eight years of school," he snickered at me.
"All we did was distract you." His face was slightly flushed
from drinking too much. "Can't help it. After this long, I
can't let you lose touch because we grew up."

"I wouldn't want to." I took a deep breath and patted his hand. "Let's go home."

It took us a moment to stumble out to the curb, and after a little debate, we shared an Uber back to my apartment. We used each other as support. His scent was a mix of sawdust, oil, and musky man that would put me off if it were anyone else. With Lucas, though, it was as familiar as going home to Mama's for dinner. I turned into his shoulder and breathed him in. If this was cologne, then I wanted a bottle of it so he wouldn't take me burying my nose against his throat the wrong way.

"Priorities," he reminded me, sounding sleepy.

"S'why you're sleepin' on the couch," I murmured back.

"Good, cuz you snore." He shook as he laughed it out. "You snore loud."

"S'why you sleep on the couch." I nudged him with my elbow.

When the Uber driver cleared her throat, I jerked away from him. Lucas was quick to pull his wallet from his back pocket to tip the driver. I let him and opened the door so we could fall out. His hand gripping my elbow was the only thing that kept me from doing a less than graceful faceplant. When we got to the apartment door, I struggled with the keys to the point that Lucas just started knocking.

"Sara's asleep," I argued, trying to get him to stop.

"I gotta piss," he complained and knocked harder on the wood.

When the door opened, I tried my best to be apologetic. The fact that Lucas shoved past my roommate without a greeting didn't seem to help the sleep-deprived glare Sara gave me.

"Sorry," I hiccupped, standing out on the stoop like puppy dog eyes would save me from her wrath. I held up the messed-up keychain; there were enough keys on it that might put a janitor to shame. I jingled them at her helplessly. "I couldn't find it."

She just glowered at me, like I hadn't apologized. "Every time you go out with them, you come home drunk with one of them," she grumped at me. "All these men, people are going to start thinking we're both whores."

"'M not a whore." I shoved past her, wincing when I saw the bathroom light on. "They're just my friends. You know they don't even sleep with me, because anytime I bring one of 'em home, they end up on the couch."

"And the neighbors know that?" Sara closed the door and locked it.

"You bring home more men than I do," I started, trying to get the slur to my speech under control. "These are the same three guys." I stomped my foot as I couldn't keep the whine out of my voice. "We haven't even slept together!" She just shook her head at me and disappeared into her room. This was an argument we had on a semi-regular basis.

It was to the point that I was so ready to move out. Mama paid my rent for me, but when I began residency, I'd at least be pulling a paycheck. That meant I'd be able to get my own place. Then I wouldn't face a judgy roommate.

Lucas came out of the bathroom groaning. He didn't even acknowledge me, just flopped onto the living room couch heavily. Seeing him crash was enough to remind me of my own alcohol-fueled exhaustion. I padded back to my bedroom, picking up a pillow and a blanket on the way. At the sound of his snores, I didn't hesitate throwing the pillow at him.

Of course, aside from an exaggerated snort, he didn't make any sort of protest. Just snuggled deeper into the couch. I went to the kitchen and fished two bottles of water from the fridge. I dropped one on the floor for him and guzzled my own down. I sat on the coffee table, waiting for the eventual need to pee.

I found myself watching him as he hugged my pillow as if it were a stuffed animal. His face looked relaxed in a way I didn't see often. Even with easygoing moments like meeting at the bar, there was a certain type of guarded look on his features. His blond hair was tousled in a way that made me want to run my fingers through it.

"Priorities," he murmured. That's when I noticed he wasn't exactly asleep.

"What are yours then?" I asked.

"Keeping you in my life." His voice was hoarse, and his brows furrowed. Aside from the shift in his features, he still looked as if he were asleep. "That's what's important to me," it came out in a whisper.

"I'm not going anywhere," I whispered back.

2

Twelve years old

"It's a natural part of being a woman," Mama said like she was quoting the video the PE teacher made the girls watch while the boys played basketball. "This means…" She was seated beside me on my bed, going on like the history teacher. It was hard to focus on what she was saying. "It means you're well on your way to becoming a woman."

I didn't even have boobs yet, not that I wanted them. It seemed like they were the key to making boys dumb if Bryce's marveling over Casey Dawson's over-the-summer growth was anything to deduce from. If anything, waking up to bloody sheets was just another reminder of how different I was from the rest of my friends.

What would happen now? There was no more pretending I was just another one of the boys.

"This would be easier for you to understand if you had more girlfriends," Mama said, not hiding the fact she was irritated by my choice of company. "Those heathens you run around the neighborhood with won't understand what you're going through. Before too long, they'll be less interested in riding bikes with you and more interested in your developing body." She made a disgruntled noise. "Now I have to worry about them getting handsy." She touched my shoulder. "You will be saving yourself for marriage."

My stomach twisted, and a pain in my back seemed to echo the motion. "Please don't make this a sex talk,

Mama," I didn't bother to refrain from whining it. There'd been failed attempts at THE talk before, and I didn't want this to be another. My stomach hurt, and all I wanted to do was curl up in bed without her harping at me that the boys would be nothing but trouble.

"It's just a downward spiral from here," she kept on like she hadn't heard me. "We'll get with Pastor Bill about the importance of staying pure and abstinent. That way you'll understand why it's so important that you save yourself."

"Mama," I whined again. I didn't want to tell her that I never wanted to get married. Not after what Daddy did to her and seeing how bitter she'd become now. The only boys I could trust were those in the neighborhood, despite what she thought.

The doorbell rang, like a saving grace, and I would be sure to thank God for it when Mama dragged me to church on Sunday. "There's probably the heathens now," she grumped as she got up to answer the door.

"I don't want to play today," I admitted.

"Well, you missed school. While I'm willing to allow for one day for this, you're not going to gallivant around the neighborhood with your friends if you're going to miss school," she agreed with me. I had expected it since that was the general rule for missing school.

"I'll go to school tomorrow," I promised, though I didn't know for sure. I crawled up my bed with the intention of wallowing in the fact I wasn't a boy. There was no denying I was a girl now. Boys had it so much easier.

That's when I heard Mama talking. "She won't be coming out to play today," she said coldly. "Perhaps tomorrow. Unless Francine finally decides to grow up and stop playing in the mud."

"Is she okay?" Lucas' voice was filled with worry because that's what he did. If he couldn't look after us, he worried about us.

"She'll be fine," Mama said, still sounding mean. "Maybe she'll see you tomorrow at school." At least that was a little better. I didn't feel like getting up to make sure he didn't get his feelings hurt with her. The boys were used to Mama's attitude towards them by now. She wasn't anywhere as nice as Mrs. Wilks or Mrs. Kemp.

"Okay," Lucas' quietly replied.

I heard the front door close, and I glanced to see Mama in the doorway of my room. "Girls will understand what you're going through," she said lightly. "These boys won't do anything but turn their noses up at it." She looked sympathetic as if she were sad about what was happening to me. "It will get easier, baby. You'll get used to men disappointing you. You'll get used to dealing with this every month."

She left me there, holding onto my knees and trying to figure out just what I was gonna do from here. Especially if they figured out this monthly thing would be too much for them to deal with. My throat burned at the idea of losing my best friends. Then the tears started, and I didn't bother trying to stop them.

Why did I have to grow up when I finally felt happy?

There was a light tap at my window. At first, I ignored it, then it happened again. I looked to see Lucas there; he had squeezed behind the bushes in front of my window. His brows were down, and he waited there expectantly.

I messily wiped my face and shoved off the bed. With a little effort, I pushed my window open. "Mama said I couldn't come out to play today."

"I know." He frowned at me. "But are you okay?"

I considered him through the screen, something neither of us bothered to push out. Mama was in the other room, and even if she didn't hear him at my window, she'd hear me talking to him. Now seemed as good a time as any to break it to him, I just needed to rip the band aid off. I took a deep breath. "I started my period."

He looked at me blankly. "What?"

Mama was right. I could feel the tears falling down my cheeks. "Every month, women bleed." I paused and pointed towards my thighs, hoping the overly large pad in my panties wasn't too obvious. It felt massive. "Down there. Mama said I'm a woman now."

Lucas blinked at me, then his cheeks went red. He looked away from me and poked at the sheer screen separating us. "But you're okay, right?" His voice cracked a little when he asked, and he looked at me like he was just as embarrassed by this conversation as I was.

"It hurts," I answered honestly. Even now, standing at the window, my back ached.

"Mom has a heating pad she uses," he started, "when she gets moody. I guess it's because of that." He swallowed obviously and took a breath. "But you're gonna be okay. We can come to hang out tomorrow or if... if you don't want to ..."

"You still wanna be my friend?"

"Duh," I could hear Bryce from behind the bush. "Don't be stupid, Frank. You're one of us."

The bush shifted, and with a hiss, Noah pushed aside some of the leaves so I could see his face. "We stick together. Gonna be harder than being a girl to get rid of us." His brown eyes pinned me. "We'll see you tomorrow, yeah?"

I sniffled and nodded, happy for once that Mama was wrong. "Yeah." I wiped my cheek. "I'll be at school tomorrow." In front of my friends, I struggled not to cry. But still, the tears flowed. "Thank you," I whimpered out.

Noah gave me a slight smirk. "We deal with our moms going crazy once a month, Frankie. We can deal with you too."

"I mean…" Bryce edged in around the bush and winced at getting poked. "What are friends for?"

3

***

Present Day

When I got up the next morning, my head pounded. But after a couple of bottles of water and a few Tylenol, I felt something more human. By the time I got out of the shower, I found the couch empty. Not that it mattered. I had to get ready for my first day of residency, so not having to worry about Lucas was one less thing for me to stress about.

It didn't take me long to get ready, the benefit of scrubs. They weren't fashionable, but that was never a concern for me. What caused me to hesitate was the question as to whether I should wear makeup. I was looking forward to the next few years at this hospital, doing what it took to do what I dreamed of.

Four more years.

I opted for just a little, enough to make it look like I hadn't spent the night before drinking. *I'm not hung over.* I figured if I said that to myself enough, I'd believe it.

By the time I was ready to walk out the door, I ended up bolting back to the bathroom to heave up the contents of my stomach. Mind over matter was a thing, I believed. But it didn't help when you lost count of the number of shots you had the night before with friends. Or it could be nerves and an empty stomach.

An empty stomach was enough for me to grab a pack of snack crackers from the pantry. After my first day, I was determined to have a talk with Mama about getting my own place. I didn't like Sara guilting me for having my friends over, even when they weren't there to crash on the couch after one too many drinks. It was almost as bad as living back at home where I'd only see them when I went outside because they were never allowed to come in.

It felt like all through college I had watchful eyes on me. Despite Dad footing the bill, Mama watched to see if I would screw it all up. Like she expected the boys to lead me down a road where I'd end up pregnant and destitute, probably addicted to drugs. She didn't consider all the times I went outside with my friends, their parents opened their doors to us. Their mothers looked over all of us like we were just another one of theirs.

I saw what a healthy relationship was supposed to be like. It also gave me the drive to make sure I was there for kids who grew up in a situation like mine. Or worse. Lucas' relationship with his father was so much worse than mine. Nonexistent for reasons that involved alcoholism and fear.

While Mama was sure that I would mess up because I hung out with boys, their moms knew I had it in me to prove her wrong. I had a strong support system, even if Mama wasn't included in it.

Now, I felt confident going to the hospital I was to be a resident at… even after throwing up.

Nerves, it had definitely been because of nerves.

That confidence kept going with me when I stood with my soon-to-be fellow doctors. It kept me going through the line as we were given a tour and met head nurses. It was a whirlwind of faces and names I wouldn't remember. By the time we were given a lunch break, which came with a warning that it wouldn't be like this tomorrow, I found my way down to the cafeteria.

I stood in line at the buffet with a tray in hand; a club sandwich, chocolate pudding, and an apple. I waited patiently to pay. I had an awkward feeling in my gut, like I was back in high school. The cafeteria was a mixture of doctors, nurses, and patient families... not students. It wasn't hard to discern who was who with the difference of plain clothes and scrubs, plus there was a seriousness around the patient families that didn't translate over to the people who worked in the hospital.

It was sobering; people came to hospitals for help, and their loved ones were left waiting for results. The last time I was here, Lucas' mother had an aneurysm a few years ago. Mrs. Porter was always a nice lady, even if I'd never gotten the chance to know her. I remembered sitting in the waiting room with him, waiting to see if there was any chance of a miracle, only to come away with a numb feeling when the news was grim.

The memory gave me a sudden need to call Mama, just to check to make sure she was okay. I wanted to hear her voice, even if it didn't have anything nice to say. Still, she would expect a full report on my first day, and I would get the relief of knowing she was still okay. Judgy, but okay.

"Look who it is," Bryce's voice boomed from behind me, knocking me out of the melancholy mood. His arms wrapped around my shoulders and tugged me back into his barrel chest. "Frankie," he sounded genuinely pleased to see me. "What are you doing here?"

"I know I told you my residency was here." I struggled not to topple over or drop my tray of food. I managed an elbow into his ribs, and he loosened his hold on me. "What are you doing here?"

"Physical therapy." He sounded too thrilled when he told me. "It's my jam. I started working here after I got my licenses about six months ago. I told you last night." He nudged me as he spoke. "I spend my own money."

"We were being assholes," I relented and moved with the line. I knew for a fact that, despite what he might say on the matter, B hadn't grown up much. Even after college and getting closer and closer to thirty, I knew he still had the mentality that he was supposed to get everything he wanted. He owned that sense of entitlement that the older generations thought we all had.

B gave me a smile and a shrug, suggesting he was used to the treatment. "Wanna have lunch together?"

I nodded, suddenly feeling relieved to see him. "I was just having a throwback to high school. All that was missing was you guys."

Bryce's smile widened into his usual grin. "Give me warm fuzzies, Frankie. I'm gonna get me some chow. Find a seat, and I'll come find you."

I nodded again in agreement. The nervousness I'd been awash with now gone with a familiar face, I found a tiny booth by the window, the view being of the smoking area. With as easily amused as Bryce could be, I was sure he'd treat it as if they were animals in a zoo for us to watch. When he plopped in the chair across from me, he proved that, chomping on a chip to peer out the window to eye the smokers.

"I didn't know you worked at Mercy," I prodded, getting his attention.

"You've been busy." He shrugged like there wasn't a point to discuss it. "Plus, you had that guy keeping you distracted. It didn't seem important to mention that I'd gotten a job and decided to try being an adult." He leaned onto the table to eye me as I dug into my sandwich, "Not to take away from you guys being assholes, because you are. But you're my assholes. Like you not mentioning you were working here. That's a serious foul play, Frank."

"I mentioned it," I huffed at him. Though I wasn't sure if I'd said it to Bryce specifically. We hadn't chatted one on one for a little while. But I was fairly certain I'd put something in our group text. I was trying to resist the urge to pull my phone out to check. "I think…" I swallowed as I had to concede that part to him. I honestly couldn't remember. "Maybe you were too busy chasing skirt to remember."

"I don't chase girls," he snorted as he went back to his own lunch. "They chase me." His lips twitched up in a slight smirk.

I didn't bother to refrain from rolling my eyes. Bryce was definitely nice to look at with his high cheekbones and carefree grin, I couldn't deny him that. But he was never one to commit.

"Yeah, well, we're getting old. At some point, you have to stop being chased and let one catch you for more than a minute."

"When the right girl," his gaze met mine as he spoke, "starts the chase, it'll happen. She just hasn't, yet."

I paused, mid-bite, to look at him. He was saying something without being direct. Which was odd, since he wasn't the passive-aggressive type. I put my sandwich down and looked at him as I took the slow route to dissect what he was saying. I didn't want to assume anything, but…

"Are you wanting me to chase you?"

His brows went up like he was surprised. I knew him better than half the girls he paraded around the group when we got together. But now, I wasn't sure if I caught him off guard, or I was just reading too much into his words. He rolled his shoulders and relaxed back into the bench. "I mean, if you wanna piece of this, Frankie, all you gotta do is ask."

It struck me speechless.

Bryce flirted with any woman he crossed paths with, but there always seemed to be something unspoken between us. I was treated like one of the boys for so long, I didn't expect this. I blinked at him, trying to come up with something so I didn't look stupid just staring blankly.

"I didn't think you," I started then stopped myself. I didn't want to give him the impression that I thought about any of them in a more than friendly way. Even though I did so on the occasion when I was alone, no other man in my life ever seemed to measure up.

I held up a hand between us, like he would come across the table and pounce on me in a busy cafeteria. He just sat there, watching me react. There was none of his usual smugness, no smartassery, just a careful blankness. It was like he was trying really hard to not react to me.

I felt like I was suddenly on the spot. I cleared my throat. "Priorities." It was an echo from Lucas the other night. "I don't know how something like this would go over. And…" I realized then he'd been right. "I wouldn't want to create a problem. We've been friends for this long…"

That careful blankness twitched. "Been talking to Lucas."

I rolled my eyes. "I talk to all three of you."

"Not about sex," he pointed out. "Not about being more than friends. Where was your guy last night?" He was pushing buttons and making a point I didn't like. He stayed kicked back like he already knew the answer, and I gritted my teeth to try to keep from looking angry.

"Some things are more important than sex," I snapped finally.

"And with some people, the sex could be fucking fantastic, but you won't know until you give in and give 'em a try," he shot back nonchalantly.

I didn't like it, especially because it was ruffling feathers and raising a good question. Growing up, I found myself looking at the three boys in my life in the same manner I looked at others. I just never had it in me to say something, to try for something more.

"Some things," I stood up, my lunch forgotten, "are just more important than sex." I picked up my tray to trash what was left on it.

I didn't even get to eat my pudding. I couldn't stomach it now.

I was out of the cafeteria and on my way to the elevator when Bryce finally caught up to me.

"Look," he looked irritated and worried, "I'm not being an asshole about this. You brought it up; I'm just being honest."

I pinched the bridge of my nose, I still had five hours before I was free to think about it. "B," I sighed as I tried to keep from looking at him. I didn't want him as temptation. "Having you in my life is more important than five minutes of sex." It was a rehash of what Lucas had said to me, and I knew, without a doubt, he was right. "Besides, why would you want to risk being a rebound?"

"It's only a rebound if you're one and done." He released a breath and looked like he'd just caught a canary. "And if all you're getting is five minutes, babe, then it's a good thing you dropped the loser." He raised his hands suddenly like he realized he was playing with fire. "Think about it. It's all I'm saying."

I hit the button to the elevator. "I'll think about it when you do."

***

Despite the weariness of the conversation I had with Bryce, I found that I had missed him. Even when he was being a pain in the ass. It didn't take him long to figure out the routine they had me started on, or the shift I was working. Of course, having lunch with him on the regular was impossible with as busy as I was after the first day.

Hospitals were busy. There were rounds, there was double checking charts, and you had to stay on your toes when faced with dire moments. It was almost enough to make me doubt myself. It was so much, and I had only just started. There were another four years of this before I could actually begin what I'd started all of this for. I started to think that I couldn't handle ten-plus hours for the next four years of my life. We hadn't even started a night shift, but I knew it was approaching.

I sat on the bottom bunk of one of the on-call rooms, rubbing my fingers into my temples in a vain attempt to keep myself from cracking. I couldn't quit, but the question as to whether I could hack this was there.

I heard the door open but didn't bother to look up. I had my face cupped in my hands, and I was trying to find some sort of second wind to keep me going. The bed I sat on dipped.

"Brought you coffee," B whispered from beside me.

It was like God had put angel wings and a halo on him. He'd never been so beautiful to me in my life. I took the liquid gold from him and took a careful sip of the hot liquid. It already had sugar in it, along with a splash of creamer, just enough to take an edge off the bitterness. I didn't hold back my groan as I continued to drink it.

"Been rough?" He kept his voice low as he asked, peering around the room curiously. I hadn't checked to see if it were empty or not when I walked in. I'd just gone to a bed and collapsed.

"Thought I was ready to get to the hard part of being a real doctor," I said between sips. "I might have overestimated my abilities."

"Nah." He watched me with a slight smile. "It just takes time for you to adjust. By the time you get a day off, you'll be exhausted beyond comprehension. But you'll have time to recoup."

"I guess it's a good thing I'm single." I released a sigh, not thinking as I said it. "Nobody to disappoint when all I need to do is sleep."

His features twitched, and he raised an eyebrow. "When's your day off?"

"Tuesday." I went back to the coffee like it had called my name. "Gonna miss our weekly night out." I already felt bad about it. I gave him a look, expecting some sort of whining from him, only to be surprised.

Bryce sat beside me with an understanding look on his face. "We knew it was coming. We gotcha, Frankie. Just holler when you need coffee, and I'll bring it to you." The way he said it, hushed as if it were a secret between us, did something to me I couldn't explain.

I looked at him, trying to figure out if this was just my friend striving to be a good friend... Or if this had something to do with the conversation from the other day. He wanted more, I knew that, but from the sincerity I saw on him now, it might be that he wanted more than just sex.

"Figure out how to get this into an IV, and I'll owe you one," I joked. It seemed like the safest thing to do; I didn't want him to realize what I was thinking about. "More than one," I added because I could already feel the little bit of a caffeine buzz kicking in. It'd probably only last me an hour, but I could find a way to get more when I drooped again.

"I'm on it." He grinned at me. "I'm done for the day, but if you need food or whatever," there was a glance back at the beds of the on-call room, "feel free to call me."

I nodded and promised, "I'll be sure to bring you coffee on my day off."

"My job is a whole lot easier than yours." He stood and looked down at me with his usual swagger. "I didn't dream as big as you did." It didn't sound like bragging, but because this came from Bryce, that's what I took it as.

I took a final sip of my coffee, maneuvering my hands so I could give him a proper one-fingered salute while I emptied the cup. He snorted in amusement and left me to face the rest of my shift. It left me feeling better at least.

Somewhere between the studying of symptoms, looking at charts, and worrying about screwing up, I had a thought. *Why couldn't I just think about it? Why couldn't I look at Bryce, or any of the other guys, appreciatively?*

4

<hr />

Fourteen years old

"Did you get the invite to Casey Dawson's party?" Bryce's voice cracked a little bit over the phone. "It's a party for boys and girls!" There was an excitement in his voice that fed over the line. "Did you get an invitation, too? Noah and Lucas did! Mom said she was gonna let me go if the rest of you were going. Lucas is going; his mom is always cool about letting him go to birthday parties, and Noah is already working his mom for a 'yes.' The only one I know is iffy is you."

I winced, trying to think of the best way I could break it to him. Aside from the fact that Mama probably wouldn't let me go, Casey didn't like me very much. "I didn't get an invitation," I tried to be gentle about it. I figured it was because she was jealous. From the sound of it, I was the only one in our group of friends who didn't get an invitation. She must have liked one of them and thought I was in the way.

"What?" His excitement went from sixty to zero fast. Like I threw a bucket of cold water on him.

"I'm sure if your mom knows that Noah and Lucas are going, you can still go." I shrugged like he could see me.

He was quiet for a beat. "Why wouldn't she invite you?"

"I don't know," I lied, not wanting to tell him about the catty remarks the other girl made about how I dressed too much like a boy, how I would never get a boyfriend that way, and that I was probably gay. "Don't worry about it. You guys have fun."

Bryce made a disgruntled noise, "Come outside. We need to have a meeting." He hung up, not waiting to see if Mama would let me out this late.

I sighed and got up out of bed, Mama was in the kitchen, cleaning up after dinner, and I was supposed to be doing homework. She stood at the sink, humming a hymn from church that I vaguely recognized. "Mama," I tried to sound stern, "I'm gonna go out to the front lawn. Bryce's having problems with his algebra homework. I'm gonna see if I can help him out. Okay?" It was a lie, a white lie, but I thought it she would be less likely to object if she knew I was helping him.

She gave me a glance, something on her face making me doubt she'd let me to it. Then she nodded at me. "Stay in the yard where I can see you."

I wanted to protest, a rebellious thought wanting to argue that I wasn't a baby, but I tamped it down hard. If I objected, Mama would send me to my room, and any chance of anything happening from here would be lost.

"Yes'am. Thanks, Mama." Respect would get me a whole lot farther than the need to have some independence.

I hurried out the front door, giving the front window one last glance before I went to the end of the yard. "Bryce," I called out and waved when I saw him standing under the streetlight.

He waved back and trotted my way. I heard a door open and saw Noah wandering over. Lucas was quieter about it, and if it weren't for the streetlights, he probably would've gotten the drop on us. I gave the house behind me a glance. I saw Mama in the window with her watchful eyes narrowed.

Well, I won't be able to use the homework lie again.

"Casey didn't give her an invite," B reported as we all met up in front of my house. "I'm pretty sure if Frank doesn't go, Mama's not gonna let me go." He waved a hand back in his house's direction. "She seems to think Frank is gonna keep me out of trouble."

"What does she think is gonna happen?" Noah asked, his voice going a little high on the end of that question. "That we're gonna get into drugs and alcohol? I can barely talk without sounding like a screech owl. I'd like to be able to have a full conversation without this shit happening." He sounded more than a little irritated as his voice cracked.

"You and me both," Lucas groaned.

"I'd like to get the opportunity to kiss a girl," Bryce snapped. "Dad's making me try out for junior varsity football. The only boob I'm gonna see that's not on the internet is hers." He waved a hand at me. "I'd like to see some that I might actually stand a chance at touching."

"Cop a feel, and I'm gonna break your hand," I threatened, folding my arms over my breasts. I didn't have much to offer, but it always seemed to throw me off kilter when they took notice of them. "I don't see why it matters that I go."

"I don't see why Casey didn't invite you," Lucas started. "When she gave me the invitation, she made out like everyone would be there. Maybe she forgot to give you yours? Did you check your locker?"

Lockers were a new concept I was still getting used to. We had them in middle school, but I had so little use for them, I never bothered. The boys, of course, enjoyed the concept of them and would often drop notes into girls' lockers that they had crushes on. I didn't realize it was a thing until the end of eighth grade when there was a small pile of folded papers in my locker. Some of them were just random notes, and some were from 'secret admirers' that were in a familiar script. Since I never spoke about them, they figured I had written off the idea of lockers in favor of lugging around an overloaded book bag for another year.

Freshman year wasn't as easy to balance as eighth grade, not with the advanced classes that Mama insisted I take. "I checked," I assured him after a beat. "She didn't invite me because she doesn't like me," I clarified for them and shrugged helplessly. "I don't need to go. You guys go. Have fun."

I got a bunch of sour looks. Lucas just folded his arms over his chest, mirroring my stance and eyeing me in a way I didn't like. He was plotting something. Noah 'oh man'd' and turned away, like he was ready to call the meeting and head back home. Bryce flopped down on the grass and picked at it like he was ready to wait out me changing my mind.

"Besides," I decided to point out the most obvious thing, "Mama would never let me go, especially if she knew the boys were gonna be there." I cast another glance back at the house to see her sitting in the living room. It looked as if she were watching television, but I knew better.

"Tell her you got an invitation." Lucas finally broke his suspicious look. "It's a girl's party; don't mention that we'll be going."

"You're telling me to lie?" I was surprised, considering Lucas played so carefully with my mother. He respected her even though it was clear she had no love for any of the three boys in my life. "What happens when I get caught? How do you expect me to get there without her? She'd find out then."

"Maybe you could call her and ask her if you could come?" B had a hopeful tone to his voice. "Say please and don't be an asshole about it. There's no reason why she'll say no. When you act nice, Frankie, people like you."

"I'd rather not have to act, and I'd rather be me." I shrugged at him "I'm not girly enough for Casey. Why is this an issue?"

"Because," Bryce got up and was suddenly in my face, "we do everything together! We're best friends! It's our first high school party! Why can't you just suck it up?"

"Or just crash the party," Lucas offered. "They do it in movies all the time." He rubbed at the back of his neck as he spoke. "There's no reason she would say anything. We just need to work on your mom." After he said it, his attention was directed towards my house. The rest of our attention followed.

Mama seemed to be focused on the television. I knew she was actually watching us, but I was sure we were far enough away that she wouldn't hear us. "I doubt there's much of anything that'll get her to agree to let me go," I admitted without looking away. "We're lucky she let me camp out in your backyard in fifth grade," I directed at Bryce.

"What if my mom talks to her? She likes her," B offered. "I can run and get her to call her on the phone."

"You can try it," I sniffed doubtfully. "Just tell 'em that I won't be able to go because they know how Mama is."

Like she knew what I said, Mama stood and came to the front door. She opened it and gave us a disdainful look. "That's enough with homework help."

"Mrs. Moore." Bryce stepped around me. There wasn't any sort of apprehension in his voice; he walked with a confidence I didn't know he had. "There's a party Friday night, and we want Frankie to go." He made it a demand, probably how he talked to his own parents.

I could see something twitch on Mama's features, like she was offended, but she didn't want to show it. It was something I'd seen a few times when we'd gotten in an argument. Her face would twitch before closing up tighter than hurricane shutters before she laid down the law.

"Francine hasn't mentioned it to me," she said evenly. There was steel in her voice that made me swallow. "But give us time to discuss it, and we shall see. Good night." She gave me a look then, her eyes connecting with mine in an unspoken command.

"Night, guys," I murmured quietly as I turned around to go in.

Mama closed the door after me, and I waited for her to lay the 'no' hammer down on me. "What do you know about this party?" She sounded reasonable when she asked, taking me by surprise.

"One of the popular girls in our grade is throwing it. I think she's a cheerleader or something," I tried to sound nonchalant about it as I struggled to think about Casey. We didn't have any classes together, and she barely ever said a word to me. She would just give me the briefest of nods when I was surrounded by the boys. I just couldn't figure out which one of them she was trying to impress. "I didn't get an invitation," I told her honestly. I figured she already caught me in a lie, there was no reason to try to give her another. "Mrs. Wilks said if all of us was going, Bryce could go, too."

"You weren't invited?" She looked surprised when she said it. Mama then took the time to lock the front door before she sat on the couch and looked at me expectantly, "Why weren't you invited?"

I gave a futile look back towards my bedroom before I gave her a rundown of the nonexistent friendship I had with the girl throwing the party. "She probably didn't invite me because she likes one of the boys, and she thinks I'm competition." I shrugged helplessly.

"This is part of the problem you run into when you have nothing but friends who are boys," she said in a tone that sounded suspiciously gentle. "Perhaps you should go; you might expand your circle of friends."

I stared at her, wondering if this was a case of the body snatchers. Had my real mom been abducted and replaced with an imposter? "Are you sure?" I asked dumbly.

"You will have a curfew. I expect you to be home by ten." She stood and nodded, seemingly deciding on the fact I could have a social life. "If you come home inebriated in any fashion, we will not come to an agreement like this again. If you can prove to me that I can trust you to be responsible, then I may give you a little leniency with things such as this." She paused to turn off the living room lights. "It's a part of growing up. I'm guessing the reason for Mrs. Wilks' demand is that she trusts you to keep her boy out of trouble, isn't it?"

"Probably," I fidgeted as I answered.

"Well," Mama pressed a kiss against my forehead, "call your friend and let him know the good news. Of course, you'll need to make sure your chores and homework are all done in a timely manner before this party happens."

"Thank you, Mama." I gave her a hug. I didn't have the heart to tell her I didn't want to go. I was trapped into it now. She probably thought me going to a party like this would either show me the kind of people I should be hanging out with, or that the boys that were my friends were only after one thing.

I decided not to call Bryce when I got to my room. I went to bed with the weight of the knowledge that I would be a party crasher. And Mama encouraged it.

***

There was this temptation to dress up, to wear a skirt I reserved purely for church events Mama dragged me to, but I reconsidered. I elected to go for the newest pair of jeans I had and a plain t-shirt that was a little loose on me. I wasn't striving to make an impression; it was something I would've worn to school. It wouldn't matter what I wore, I wouldn't be welcome. I figured I might as well be comfortable.

What held me up was the question as to whether I should wear makeup. Despite what the boys might think, I did own some. I had a general idea of how to put it on. I just... I wasn't sure. After looking at my reflection for what felt like an hour, I elected for a little mascara and tried not to stab myself in the eye in the process. I then took the time to dab a little foundation on the outbreak of pimples on my chin.

I was nervous, which I hadn't expected.

I got up and stepped out of my bedroom. I was down the hallway and in front of Mama without realizing it. "Tell me I can't go," I demanded.

She paused, putting her book face down on her lap and looking up at me with only a little bit of surprise. "Why would I do that?" She stood and came to me with an expression I wasn't familiar with; it looked like it might be amusement. "You made an effort to behave and did just what I asked you to do. Why don't you want to go?" She took her time to carefully rub her thumb against my chin. "Blend a little so it doesn't stand out so much."

"The only people who like me are the boys," I confided to her. "And they're going to be interested in all the other girls who are there. So as soon as we get there, they're gonna ditch me."

"You're afraid that they'll like another girl more than you?" She had a knowing look on her face that made my stomach knot up.

"They're my friends." I sounded like a little kid who was whining because someone was playing with one of my favorite toys. "It's not gonna be any fun."

"You won't know until you go," Mama said evenly. "This is likely the only time I'll allow something like this. The older you get, the worse the parties will be. I'm sure I won't be able to trust those boys to stay honorable as they have up until now. I think…" She pursed her lips as she swiped her thumb under my left eye. "I think it'll be best that you go. Not just for the opportunity to connect with other girls, but for the chance to see where your friends' loyalties lie."

I saw then the reason she was letting me go. It sobered me to the point that I wouldn't ask again to not go. When Bryce knocked on the door, I picked up the gift I had bought for Casey. *Wuthering Heights* seemed like an appropriate gift, even though I was sure she'd probably never read it. I made one last promise to be home by ten, then left to crash my first party.

I got odd looks from the boys when I got in the car, and I noticed that they looked a little nicer than usual. B had a dress shirt on with khakis, Noah's shirt looked new, and Lucas looked as if he had put something in his hair to make it spikey. They made more of an effort than I did.

It felt like my heart was sliding into my stomach. I sat in the backseat beside Lucas, trying my best to not let myself be bothered by the fact I would have to get used to the idea of sharing them. I was sure to tell Mrs. Wilks my curfew, not that I wanted to kill the party for everyone.

They groaned anyway, but I didn't want to get in trouble for something I was sure I would hate.

The party wasn't like any other party I'd been to. There was a lot of people I recognized from my different classes, but none of them were people I'd call friends. They didn't try to connect with me, and I didn't reach out. Luckily, I didn't get a second look when I walked through the door with my friends, and no one told me to leave.

Music pounded somewhere, some popular pop music I didn't know the name to. Not that I didn't like it, it just wasn't something we usually listened to. We moved through the open house, seeing people drift around the living room and into the kitchen. I didn't see her parents until we followed the train of people. Casey's mom was an extreme opposite of mine. She was dressed like her daughter and offered us drinks from red cups before directing us down to the basement.

The music was louder downstairs. People danced awkwardly on one side of the broad room, and a group near the stairs sat in a circle, laughing. The closer we got, the better I could see what they were doing. There was a bottle in the center, and just as it whirled to a halt, I watched as two people met in the middle to kiss. I felt heat rush to my cheeks, and I looked away. "Spin the bottle? Really? What are we, twelve?"

"What's the matter, Moore?" Casey perked up from the circle. "You don't wanna kiss boys? Like girls instead?" There seemed to be a moment of silence for that well thought-out jab, and I didn't resist the urge to roll my eyes.

Casey liked to either straight-out say I was gay or imply it. I guess it was better than her calling me a slut or a whore. I didn't like the idea of sharing my boys, but I didn't like the idea of people thinking I was doing something with them.

"I thought this was supposed to be the first high school party of the year," I spoke up as each of the boys I was with eagerly found a spot in the circle. "Or are we still in middle school?"

"If you want, you can kiss girls instead of boys," Casey continued as she grinned at me. "I mean we didn't have a rule for it, but we can give the complete understanding that if it's your spin, and it lands on a girl, they have to kiss you."

"Just sit," Bryce whined at me.

"You keep talking like this, Dawson, and I'm going to think you have a crush on me," I shot at Casey, trying to go for a mocking tone as I sat next to Noah. "You catch more with honey than you do with vinegar." I just hoped my bravado wouldn't be interpreted as anything more than just talk.

"I didn't use any honey, and here you are." She made a face as she said, "What are you doing here?"

"Everyone else is here from our grade," Lucas spoke up. He sat across from me, and he directed a dark look at Casey. "What'd you do? Forget to give Frankie an invitation? Or did you just not want her to come, too?"

Casey's face went red, and she fidgeted before shoving the bottle towards me. "It was an accident," she said lowly to Lucas. "But she came with you guys, so it fixes that, right? Here, Frankie." She pulled my name harshly. "Why don't you go first?"

I grimaced, but I grabbed the bottle and reached forward with it in the middle. I was about to lose my first kiss in the stupidest of ways. I twisted the bottle and let it whirl. It spun as I drifted back to the place I'd claimed on the floor. I watched the bottle spin with a growing sense of dread.

It slowed down, then skidded to a stop. There was a chorus of ohs that made my stomach twist. I wasn't ready to see who it pointed at. I swallowed a lump and looked to see who was on the other side of the bottle.

Bryce stared at me wide eyed, with his mouth slightly agape. He shot a helpless look to Lucas, and I mirrored the action. What were we supposed to do? Kiss?

All Lucas did was shrug.

I edged forward, and Bryce came to meet me. His breath hitched, and he pressed his face close to mine. I didn't know the mechanics of how to do this, so I tilted my head and pressed my lips hard against his. He made a choked noise and pulled away. His face was bright red, and he backpedaled to the place he had claimed.

I felt all eyes on me. Instead of sitting back, I got up and went back upstairs. No one said a word or tried to stop me. I went through Casey Dawson's house until I got to the front porch. I sat heavily on the first step and tried to remember to breathe.

Did I regret it? Was it bad that my first kiss was with Bryce?

I didn't know. But I was willing to bet I was the butt of everyone's jokes downstairs.

I heard the door creak open behind me and the stumbling steps out onto the wood porch. I didn't look to see who was behind me. I felt my heart beating heavily; the sound of it throbbed in my ears.

"Go away," I snapped without care to who it was.

"I don't want to." Bryce's voice was quiet. He sat beside me. I felt the nervous energy coming off him in waves. I didn't bother to look. "I'm sorry."

"What for?" I snorted like this wasn't a big deal. Like it didn't bother me when it did. I didn't know what to think or how to feel. I'd never looked at Bryce that way, and I wasn't prepared to do that now.

"Was it your first kiss?" He sounded uneasy when he asked it.

I didn't answer, but I glared angrily at the Dawsons' front yard. There was a ring of light from the porch, and I could see the carefully manicured green grass and the pretty sidewalk with its colored pavers. I didn't want to see Bryce's flushed face. The view I had now was better.

"It was mine." His voice sounded so small. "I'm sorry it was bad."

"Go back inside," I snapped. "This was the party you just had to come to. So go enjoy it."

"I don't want to," Bryce said softly.

I swallowed hard but couldn't think of any other argument to get him to go away. We sat, just the two of us, until his mom got there. She was about ten minutes early, and I never loved Mrs. Wilks more at that moment. If it weren't for the fact I had a curfew, I would've liked nothing more to be in the comfort of her presence.

But Mama was waiting for me.

I found her in the living room with her knitting in her hands. She gave me a warm smile, something that seemed out of place. Maybe it was the fact I was in a mood and wanted nothing but to go to bed.

"Did you have fun?" she prompted, setting what she had been working on down in its basket. "Come tell me how it was."

"I'd rather go to bed," I told her honestly.

"Oh?" She didn't look surprised. "Did something happen? Did 'your boys' do as I expected them to do?" The way she asked it held something I couldn't put a name to. But looking at her face, I was able to. Smug. She looked smug.

I didn't know what she expected; I could only imagine what she thought happened. I didn't want to tell her about giving my first kiss to Bryce. I took a breath and did my best to put on a brave face.

"No," I said with an effort to be stoic. "I'm going to bed."

Surprisingly, she let me go.

5

Present Day

I could hear a knock at the door, but I had my head buried so far under my pillow, it'd take an excavation crew to get it out. I didn't want to move. I was too comfortable in my bed, and the prospect of doing anything outside of staying curled up burrito style was off the table. Fortunately, Mama paid the bills, and all I ever needed to do was eat, study, and get good grades. Now that tuition was taken care of, she insisted that I focus on making it through residency and not worry about the little things like rent.

As of right now, the salary I made went into a savings account for when I finished this leg of my education, to work my way into becoming a practicing child psychiatrist. Mama was supportive of the idea. It seemed like the smart way to go, especially if she was willing to keep paying my bills.

I say she was paying them, but it was Dad. We didn't talk much; he only did the occasional phone call. But he kept up paying child support long after the fact I'd outgrown it. While he hadn't been keen on being a family man, he had taken the time to set aside money for me to go to college.

It made life easier for me, but it didn't keep people from knocking at the apartment door. I didn't bother to get up. I was cool with just rolling over and ignoring the knocking. That didn't mean Sara wasn't above answering the door.

I heard her talking and then the voice of our visitor. I didn't even consider who it might be until there was a tap at my bedroom door. I grunted, something close to 'go away,' and it went ignored.

"I come bearing gifts," Bryce boomed too loud like he knew I was asleep. "Coffee and bagels. C' mon, sleeping beauty. It's time for you to get up."

"It's time you take a long walk off a short pier," I grumbled, not even bothering to give him a glance.

"Frankie," he 'tsk'd and sat on my bed, reaching forward to place a cup of coffee on my nightstand. "You gotta adapt to the work schedule." He set the bag of what I assumed to be bagels beside the coffee. "Eventually, you'll get used to it. You just can't go all comatose when you get a day off. Don't you got shit to do?"

"I got sleep to catch up on, and you're interrupting that." I yawned and burrowed deeper into my blanket burrito.

"C' mon." He slapped my hip, somehow finding it under the sheet and blanket. "We're adults now, kid. We can't stay in bed all day anymore."

"Speak for yourself. Don't you have a job you should be at?" I tugged the blanket down enough so I could see him clearly. I'd been lying on my side, and I shifted so I was curled to him. "Why are you here?"

"Breakfast." He pointed like it was the obvious thing. "Friendship? The chance to see what kind of mess you live in now that your mom doesn't ride you about cleaning the house?" B glanced around my room, taking in the piles of laundry before looking back at me. "What're you gonna do when you run out of clothes?"

"Are you waiting to see if you can catch a chance to see me naked?" I raised an eyebrow at him.

He tried to look innocent before shrugging and nodding. "I mean... sure, why not." He eyed the pile of dirty scrubs. "Or I could be offering you help with it? If I get an eyeful in exchange, that seems fair."

I groaned and finally give in, grabbing a handful of his shirt so I could heft myself up into a sitting position. I then reached for the coffee he brought and took a whiff of it. "What're you doing, B?" I asked before giving the paper cup a sip.

He grimaced at me, eyeing me with my bedhead and no-makeup face. "I'm trying," he said after a few heartbeats. "You make fun of how I am with women, and I'm trying to make it clear that I'm not that way with the woman I want."

"But..." I took a moment to rub the sleep from my eyes. "Bryce... how do you expect something like this to go over with everyone else?" I tried to run my hand through my hair, only to get a fist full of tangles. "You guys have been more family to me than my actual family. I don't want to destroy the foundation that's keeping me afloat." I took a breath, and I could see my words affecting him in a way I didn't want; no one ever took rejection well. "I won't lie and say I've never thought about it, that I didn't feel something that wasn't more than friendly towards you. But I don't want to lose anyone in the process of it all."

"Since Derek," he began, startling me with the name. Derek had been such a brief time in our lives, I never expected Bryce to remember it. "Lucas has beat into our heads that we were to keep our hands to ourselves. You were our friend, and we wouldn't take advantage of you." He took a breath and pinned me with those deep-brown eyes. "I don't want to take advantage of you. I don't want to just get a taste and leave it like that." He started to close the distance between us. "I just want a chance." I didn't try to stop him as he pressed his lips to mine, and I didn't pull away either.

I let him kiss me, brushing the seam of my lips with his tongue. I drowned in the scent of a cologne I didn't know the name of and Bryce. The smell of sweat and the bite of coffee was just underlying whatever he splashed on himself before he came here. He was making an effort for me, and it was hard to ignore, especially when he pulled away and pressed his brow to mine. His eyes were clenched closed, and I couldn't figure out what was going through his head. He was usually so easy to read, and here he was, pulling me into unknown territory.

Why couldn't I give in again?

I licked my lips and brushed my nose against his. I hadn't even brushed my teeth yet, and I was considering this. Fuck it. This was what he got for waking me up. I cupped his face with my hands and tilted him just enough so I could kiss him back. He made a noise as I took the initiative, tasting his lips and pressing forward to swipe my tongue against his.

He groaned a little, telling me that my morning breath wasn't as much a deterrent for him as it should've been. I pulled away, and he went to follow me, clearly not done kissing me. I stopped him by tightening the hold I had on his face.

"Tell me something." I somehow found a thought outside the sound of my heart pounding in my ears. "If you saw me kissing Lucas or Noah like this, how would it make you feel?"

He considered me a moment, his pupils large and telling that he probably wasn't thinking with the right head at this moment. He swallowed hard. "I'd probably wonder when it was my turn."

I snorted out a laugh and let go of him. "You've made a good argument. Let me think about this before I do something I regret."

Bryce took a sharp breath and leaned in again. I thought he was going in for another kiss, and I couldn't find it in me to stop him. Instead, he just hovered close. Teasing me. "You wouldn't regret anything with me." His voice was low, and I felt something inside me twist up. A man's voice shouldn't do things like that to a woman.

6

Eighteen years old

I'd lost track about how far I walked by the time I saw the entrance to the neighborhood. Noah's house was just in view, and I broke a little. There was a burning between my thighs that was only a memory of five minutes I could never get back. A memory of rough hands on my breasts and a mouth that couldn't stop drooling all over me. How Derek had gone from being a good kisser to something so messy, I'd never know. I couldn't have been more disappointed when he finished in what felt like three choppy thrusts and lazily flopped back in the seat.

I could've had him bring me home, I should've. But I couldn't be in the car with him anymore. I heard so much hype about how good sex could be, and here I felt awful, wishing I hadn't agreed to it. I should've known better, especially growing up with a bunch of boys and being familiar with their inability to have any bit of control.

Was that what sex was? Disappointment?

I stopped in front of Noah's house, unable to keep from wobbling anymore. My breath hitched, and I thought about all the lies I'd heard. There didn't seem to be anything enjoyable about it.

And they made such a big deal about losing their virginity. Mine was gone now, and there was no going back.

"Frankie?" I jerked to attention and looked at Noah's house. It was the 'mom voice.' Not my mom, but still that voice. Mrs. Kemp stood out on her porch, her arms folded over her chest, and everything about her stance made it look like she was ready to fuss. "Baby girl, what are you doing out at this hour? Your mama is gonna have a fit. I'd have a fit if you were mine, and I'm considering claiming you right now so I can set your butt straight."

"I had a date." I sniffled, then fought to reel myself in. I rubbed my face in a vain attempt to appear as if I weren't crying in her front yard.

"Baby." Mrs. Kemp was off the porch before I'd managed to straighten myself up. "Are you okay? Why didn't he drop you off? Why," her voice raised as she continued her line of questions, "are you walking home?" Mrs. Kemp wasn't a mom to trifle with.

I floundered. I didn't have the answer immediately available, and I could see from the look on her face that she put together what was wrong on her own. "Noah!" Mrs. Kemp looked like she was ready to go on a warpath. "Get your ass out here right now, boy."

Noah was out the door and in front of his mother faster than I could register. His mom didn't ask in this voice, she made demands. I'd seen her like this before, and the last time, Noah had been grounded for a month. She had found a condom wrapper on his bedroom floor, and it was something we all heard about because there'd been a talk about safe sex for everyone.

Except me, of course. I was told to save myself for marriage because it was the right thing to do. I didn't do that, and I now found myself wishing that I had. As it stood right now, if marriage meant I'd have to have sex again, then I definitely wasn't into the idea of getting married.

"What, Mama?" Noah looked from her, terrified, then to me, and his expression changed. "Frankie?" He went around his mother like she wasn't a ticking time bomb and came to me. His brows were down and his face serious. "What's wrong?"

"She just told me she was walking home from a date," his mother said angrily. "Did this boy put his hands on you, Frankie? Because I'm five seconds from calling the police and making sure that boy regrets even looking at you funny."

I closed my eyes. She thought Derek raped me. A laugh bubbled up out of me, then another. I ended up choking on a hiccup.

"No." I took a deep breath, and I let it out, trying to stop the quiver I felt my lip doing. "I wanted it," I assured her, or I tried to. I shrugged helplessly at her. "I just thought it would be better than that."

The five-alarm fire in Mrs. Kemp's eyes went out, and I saw her shoulders relax. "I was ready to tear up some boy that ain't even mine." She came to me and wrapped her arms around me, holding me tightly. "Oh, baby," she soothed as the hiccup made another bout of tears wobble to the surface. "Was that your first time?"

I nodded against her chest, taking comfort in Noah's mom. She wasn't shaming me like I knew my mother would. She held me and shushed me like she understood what I was going through. "Baby," she brushed her hand through my hair, "teenaged boys don't know anything about girls."

"Mom," Noah objected from beside us.

"They're so selfish," she continued like she hadn't heard his complaint. "You need to tell me this boy's name so I can beat some sense into him. He shouldn't have let you walk home."

"I couldn't look at him." I sniffled. "I just wanted to come home."

"It was that bad?" She pulled back to look at me. "You won't be upset if I have Noah teach him some manners?"

I laughed then, suddenly feeling better with the idea that she would be okay with him getting into a fight like that. Mrs. Kemp had a tight leash on Noah; he got straight As and stayed out of trouble. The only time she loosened it was for us: me and the other boys.

"No." I took a deep breath and let it out shakily as I held onto her. "I don't want him to get into trouble."

"Girl, you know I already claimed you." She pressed a kiss to my forehead. "Noah, walk her home. Show her how a gentleman is supposed to do things. We'll talk about this boy tomorrow."

"Mama can't know this happened." I pulled away from Mrs. Kemp then. "Please don't tell her about it."

I saw a flash of disapproval. "If she asks, I'm gonna tell her. But I'm not gonna call and give her a report," she said uneasily. "Baby, you need to have that talk with your mother. She'll tell you how it's supposed to be."

I doubted it, but I wouldn't argue with her. Not after she soothed the frazzled nerves I had. Noah wrapped his arm around my shoulders and directed me towards my house, just a little further down the street from his.

"Did he hurt you?" There was an edge to his voice like he thought I might lie to his mom. He underestimated the power his mom had on the rest of us.

"It was my first time." My lip quivered a little, and I bit down on it to stop it. "It hurt." I wouldn't tell him about the burning between my legs, or that throb that I couldn't place. I couldn't figure out why it was there.

"Did he… did he touch you there at all?" Noah looked like he was trying to be clinical about it. "Or did he just dive right in?"

"As soon as he got the condom on," I answered weakly. "The only real attention I got was bad kissing and groping like we were still freshmen."

"That fucking idiot," he sighed. "Any time a guy tries to go in without trying to finger you first is a prick, and you need to put a stop to it right there," he said it with a certainty that made me realize he knew this from practice. His face was a little darker than usual. Was he blushing? "If you don't feel wet, you don't need to let him stick anything bigger than his finger in you."

I wanted to ask him how he knew, but I could figure that out without making this conversation more embarrassing. Noah was popular among girls; they liked his dimple and the fact he was so smart. He had so much more experience than I did.

"I don't know if I can talk about this with you." I looked ahead to my house. The front porch light was on, but the other lights were off in the house. I looked harder at the front window, and I could see the glow of the TV. Mama was waiting up without making it look like she was.

I looked at my watch and saw it was twenty to ten. I wasn't late.

"It's not supposed to hurt," he said gently. "I can't speak for a girl, but I know if I do a bad job, she's probably gonna tell all her friends. Then I won't get to hit it again, and it might make it harder for me to get more." He shrugged as he turned to look at me. "Did you like him?"

I shook my head. "I didn't want to graduate a virgin. Mama hammered it in my head I need to wait for marriage. I never had the heart to tell her that wasn't something I wanted." I looked away from him because I didn't want to see any judgment from him. "He was cute, and he was interested. I just didn't think it would be that bad."

Noah shook his head and sighed. "Frankie, don't throw stuff away just because everyone else is doing it. There are plenty of guys who are interested." He kissed my cheek, and I felt my face grow hot. "I'll kick Derek's ass tomorrow. Next time you have a date that you need to escape, give me a call. That way you don't have to walk home."

"I'll remember that," I promised and smiled weakly at him. "Hopefully, it won't happen again." The only guys I would even consider seeing at this point were my guys. "Thanks for making me feel better."

"Night, Frankie." He watched as I went to the front door and unlocked it. He was still there when I went in to see Mama on the couch. I didn't see him walk home until I turned on the living room lights.

I took my time to explain that Derek wasn't the nice guy I thought him to be, and I wouldn't be seeing him again. Even though Mama thought he was upstanding, he'd played us both.

I went to bed feeling better despite the ache I still felt inside me.

***

I didn't see Derek that morning, which was a relief. There were not jeering looks or remarks about how I was easy or a slut. No one could tell my virginity was gone. It was a relief. I didn't know why it'd been a big deal from the beginning. No one would know I had sex, horribly bad sex, unless I told them.

I doubted Derek would say anything, especially after the talk with Noah. He wouldn't want me telling everyone he lasted less than five minutes.

I didn't worry about it until lunch. Usually, I had lunch with Noah and Lucas. But neither of them showed up at our usual table. Bryce was at a later period because of football practice. Lucas had work release, but he still stuck around for lunch.

Confused, I went through the snack machines, opting for a bag of chips over the sludge they were serving in the cafeteria. That's where I heard the talk. Gossip wasn't something new to lunchtime, but there was a lot of people talking about it.

"They just jumped him." I looked to see who said it. A group hung out by the snack machines, some wore black and looked like they were trying to adopt goth looks. But they were out here, away from the popular groups who hung out in the cafeteria. I figured it was so they would attract less attention. If you weren't in a popular clique, sometimes you got singled out. "All three of them," the boy said as he carefully smudged up the black eye shadow under his eyes. "Derek didn't stand a chance, and I swear I've never been so satisfied watching another guy get his ass handed to him."

"What?" I stepped closer, the bag of chips forgotten in the machine. "Who beat up Derek?"

I got a grin, and the boy who had been talking put his mirror away to give me his full attention. "You don't know? I mean they're your boyfriends, aren't they?"

"Friends," I snapped. I hated it when people assumed we were more than what we were. "I haven't seen them today. What happened?"

His lips curled upward, and he hummed primly. "Girl, if I had those three men around me all the time, I'd be claiming them before someone else did. Are they gay? Can you send one my way?"

"None of them are gay. Sorry." I shrugged helplessly at him. "Can you tell me what happened now, or do you need to string me along more?" I folded my arms over my chest, waiting to see if I needed to abandon him and find the payphone.

"They were all hauled up to the office for fighting, obviously." He rolled his eyes when it was clear I wouldn't entertain him. "Hope the no-tolerance rule doesn't get them kicked. I mean Wilks is on the football team, so he's probably safe. That doesn't say the same thing for Porter or Kemp."

I had so many questions, but I wouldn't belt them out to this guy. "Thanks." It was a weak apology, but it was all I had in me to give him.

His expression changed, and he stood up to offer me a hand. "Joseph. If any of your boyfriends decide they want to experiment, you can always give them my name. Right, Doll?"

I snorted, but I took his hand anyway. I found the pay phone near the office and dialed Noah's number after sinking a few coins into it. I knew after the conversation with his mom, he was the least likely to be in trouble.

He answered on the second ring, and I didn't give him the chance to say anything outside of a greeting. "It wasn't supposed to be all three of you!"

"It wouldn't have been," he bit back at me. "If Bryce hadn't heard him bragging. I didn't get the opportunity to head Derek off at the pass before school. I was running late this morning. But as soon as I got there, Lucas was holding him, and Bryce was using him as a punching bag." He made a noise, sounding irritated as he spoke to me. "Does this surprise you? Did you think that once they found out, they wouldn't be pissed?"

"It wasn't that serious," I tried to argue.

"Really?" he shot back. "You don't see why a guy bragging about the fact he popped your cherry would be something we'd get mad about?"

"But——" I tried to object, but he kept going.

"You're not just some rando girl at school, Frankie. If a guy is gonna talk shit like that, he's asking for it. You already knew I was gonna set him straight for letting you walk home." His voice hardened. "I needed to make sure he knew you're too special for that shit."

It left me speechless. After a talk with Mrs. Kemp, Lucas and Bryce weren't in trouble. All three moms were in the principal's office to make sure there was no chance of any of the boys getting expelled.

Somehow, through it all, I didn't get mentioned. It didn't keep me from getting looks from the other girls at school. Like they knew they had defended my honor when Derek was bragging. I decided to not confirm or deny anything. It seemed easier to leave a shadow of a doubt. If I admitted it, then Mama would surely find out. If it was just a vicious rumor, after I'd walked home from the failed date, she wouldn't believe it.

It took some stress off the situation. I wouldn't analyze Noah's words; it seemed like that would lead me down a dangerous path I wasn't sure I was ready to go down. If I had to make a choice, I knew I couldn't pick between the three of them.

They were all too important, and I wasn't willing to let any of them go.

7

***

Present Day

Having the excuse of needing to go to the laundromat was enough to get me some time to think away from Bryce and the sudden influence he had over me. I couldn't remember thinking about B sexually. Not before he slimmed down then buckled up for football. And after... any thoughts I had, I tried not to over analyze. He'd kept that frame well after he quit playing ball, and it was something I found myself thinking about as I separated my clothes. Along with the kiss he gave me this morning.

He might've been eager to help me get used to a grueling work schedule, but he wasn't keen on doing chores. That was good with me; I didn't want to fold my underwear with him watching. Plus, after I got the first load washing, it gave me the chance to make a phone call.

"S'up, doc," Noah answered after only a few rings.

"You tell me, counselor." I couldn't fight the grin that pulled across my face. "You got time to chat?"

"Working lunch," he said after a beat, then I heard him smack exaggeratedly in my ear. "I got depositions and court notes to look over to get us prepared for a date with a judge next week." After a jostle of papers, I heard a thump when he put the phone down. "Speakerphone cool with you?"

I grimaced, but I had called him at work. "I can't argue to it. Though it's kind of a personal matter that I'm calling you on." I found a chair to sit on and got comfortable for the wait.

"Let me get my earbuds out then," he said, and there was more noise from his end. "This isn't girl stuff, is it? Because I know we've had some heart to hearts, but I thought I had a little while before… that happened."

"Why is it whenever a girl wants to have a personal talk, it's always chalked up to shark week?" I didn't bother stifling my irritation as I asked.

"Yeah, yeah," he grumbled when I heard him plug something into his phone. There was a curse, then a sigh, as I could only guess he had his earbuds plugged in. "Hear me?"

"I do." I cleared my throat. "I actually called you hoping to get a piece of advice."

"I wasn't intending to go for malpractice," he answered, his voice serious. "But I might be able to pull a string or two and find you someone who can. But it's only a week, Frankie. I seriously doubt you've done anything this far to warrant needing an attorney on retainer."

"Haha," I deadpanned and glanced around the laundromat, taking in the other people cleaning their clothes. There were only two other people, and neither seemed to be paying me any mind. It didn't keep me from feeling any less awkward when I broke it to Noah, "Bryce kissed me this morning."

The line went quiet. I pulled my cell away from my ear to make sure the call hadn't dropped. "Noah?" I questioned, wondering if he heard me. I didn't want to repeat myself, but I didn't want to create an issue either.

"He kissed you." His voice was a little deeper. "When did he do this?" There was a little bit of demand in his tone.

"This morning." I was gonna be honest with Noah. There wasn't a point in calling him for advice if I glossed over the details.

"And you kicked him out?" There was something about the way he asked that I couldn't decipher.

I decided to tread carefully. "I didn't. He left after he got me rolling for the day. I have laundry to do, that's what I'm on now. You know how he is when it comes to chores." I felt uneasy now. "I didn't call to create a problem."

"You're not the one causing the problem," he snapped at me. "It's always fucking Bryce starting shit." I could hear him take a sharp breath. "There's a line we've got here, Frank. It's not the friend zone." He waited for a beat. "It wouldn't be a one and done for him. And you know how it would go down for the rest of the group."

"With B's track record, how can you be so sure he wouldn't be done as soon as we had sex?" I gave the room another cursory glance, trying to make sure I didn't have anyone's attention. "He's been a whore since Hailey Roberts gave him the time of day. Why would I be any different?"

"Because it's you," he said with finality. "You don't pour your heart out to someone for this long and be able to fuck 'em and leave 'em like that. You don't have the connection we have and do that, Frank." He groaned a little, sounding exacerbated. "What stopped you from trying to get into any of our pants before now?"

That gave me pause. It wasn't that I'd never considered it, especially whenever I turned around, they only seemed to get even more attractive. "I don't know." I struggled weakly for an excuse. "Fear of rejection? Maybe I didn't want to make things weird?"

"If that's the case, you can tell Bryce that, and he'll keep it in his pants." There was an edge in Noah's voice.

This bothered him. I was afraid to ask why. "I'll consider that. You're not upset, are you?"

"I can't be mad at you." He released a breath. "You know how Bryce can be. He thinks with the wrong head a lot and doesn't consider the consequences of his actions." He went quiet for a heartbeat or two. "It wouldn't make things weird. Well… not between us. I can't say for the other guys."

"You got plans for tonight?" I asked, deciding to change the subject to something safer.

"Right now, my plans involve putting my foot in Bryce's ass. You got a better idea?" The sarcasm in his voice was laid on pretty thick.

"Meet me at Lucas'," I suggested. "We'll talk about it as a group. Like the adults we're supposed to be. I'll bring pizza." I hoped the chance for all of us to talk it out could bring some sort of understanding. I didn't want this to be something I would just be throwing rocks at. I didn't think our friendship was fragile enough to break. "You bring the beer?" I made it a question, giving him the opportunity to shoot me down. "Can't make it a late night, though," I admitted. "Got work in the AM."

"Yeah," he said in a tone I couldn't decipher without being able to see his face. "I can bring the beer. If we're going to Lucas', we're probably gonna get stuck painting or something."

"Gotta help the man get his house in order," I barked into the phone. "You know he would do the same for you."

"You're killing me, Smalls," he grumbled. "No complaints out of me. I'll see you later tonight." He hung up after that, and it still felt strained.

Was I supposed to regret that?

I wasn't off the phone with Noah for that long before my phone was lit up with a series of texts. They were all from Bryce.

'You had to go to Noah about it?'

'Frankie, now he wants to kick my ass. If it bothered you that much, we should've talked about it.'

'It wasn't bad. I know you felt something, too.'

Of course, he was gonna assume I would take it in a bad way because I went to Noah.

'Chill out,' I sent back to him. 'We're gonna meet at Lucas'. We need to talk about it.'

'So, talk.'

'This is something that needs to be talked about with everyone. Not just between you and me.' I didn't wait for him to comment. 'I don't want to endanger anything we have going on. So either you play it cool, and I see you tonight, or you don't.'

I didn't get an immediate response, but after about an hour, I got an, 'I'll see you tonight,' while I was moving my wet clothes to a dryer. It didn't take a rocket scientist to figure out why he took so long either.

Noah had verbally ripped Bryce a new one. Hindsight had me regretting saying anything, especially since I didn't get any of the advice I was looking for.

Although I don't know what I had expected him to tell me. Maybe I wanted him to remind me of what was important in our situation.

All I could think of was the feel of Bryce's lips on mine and the taste of him.

No one called me since I had talked to Noah. I wasn't not counting the text messages from Bryce, I just figured I'd get something.

So, I would face Lucas and see what was going on in his head about all of this. I took my time getting ready, and I didn't think about what it might look like to anyone else.

"So," Sara stood in my doorway, "you finally going out with one of them?"

"What?" I had a mascara brush in hand, struggling with the decision to wear more than the bare minimum. I didn't want to give the impression I was going on a date, but I wanted them to take me seriously. Would makeup change that?

"I saw you two this morning," she said with a slight smirk. "Didn't look like just friends to me." Something in my stomach knotted up, and I looked at her. "Does this mean I can get the number to one of your other guys?"

I grimaced and went back to putting on mascara. "You can if you want to ask them for it. I don't play wingman, sorry." Even as I said it, I knew it was a lie. I'd played wingman for my boys all the time. But they were different, I trusted them to not be stupid. Even though I'd been roommates with Sara for more than a year, I didn't feel the same kind of trust with her that I did with them.

"The least you could do is share," she said grumpily as she turned around. "No reason to be greedy."

"I'm not being greedy," I hollered back at her as she left my room. I was ready to get out of the apartment and deal with what I felt. This wasn't about me being greedy. This was about finding a way to make everyone happy.

That would be, if they were open to ideas.

I took an Uber out to Lucas', both because I didn't have a car, and I intended on using liquid courage to get me through the night. I knew there'd be some objections and questions. And if things got to be too much, or I got emotional, I'd be stuck waiting for an Uber. Or worse comes to worst, I could stay at Mama's.

He did live right across the street from her, after all. His childhood home, something he got after his mom died, looked just like it always had on the outside. On the inside was another story. He spent the majority of the last year working on renovating it. I'd only seen it in various stages because he wasn't keen on having us over when he had it ripped down to the studs.

I hadn't given him much of a choice tonight. I rang his doorbell, and it made an odd noise, not much of a ring but more of croaking buzz. Lucas opened the door and gave me a look before he tapped on the button to ring the bell again.

"The hell?" He made a face and sighed.

"Wiring?" I offered, but that was about as useful as I could be when it came to things around the house. If something broke, Lucas fixed it.

"Maybe, maybe not," He shrugged. "I'll look at it tomorrow." He paused to look at me, eyeing me hard. His brows drew together, but he didn't say anything. "C' mon in." He stepped aside so I could move past him.

He'd finally hung sheetrock, and the subflooring was in. There was a ceiling fan hung and turned on as well as a floor lamp. He had four folding chairs positioned around a little flat screen set on the floor.

"You've done a lot since I was here last year," I commented because it was the truth. "Glad to see you're working towards getting it livable."

"Bathroom and bedroom were before I started stripping shit," he snorted as he led the way down the hallway. "Just, don't take off your shoes. I'm pretty sure I got all the nails and staples up, but I'd rather be safe than sorry."

I appreciated that. "Nothing fun about stepping on a nail," I commented.

I followed him to see his bedroom. The floor was an ash wood color, and at first inspection, I thought it was wood until I saw grout. It looked clean, professionally done. I knew without a doubt, he'd done it himself. It was just a piece of the craftsmanship I'd seen him capable of. He had a mattress on the floor, and the walls weren't painted, but the room was finished enough for him to live in it.

I went into the master bath. He'd taken the tile into there, and when I hit the light switch, I was pleasantly surprised with how good the room looked. It was small for a master bath, but it fit with the size of the house. He made the tiny room look like it belonged in a day spa. The sink was a bright white, surprising me with the cleanliness. The cabinet and walls were white, but the tile work of the large walk-in shower gave an impressive splash of color that left me speechless.

"Does that mean it looks good?" Lucas asked, and when I cast a glance at him, I saw insecurity on his face.

"Looks good?" I echoed and looked back into his bathroom. "Damn, man. This looks fantastic."

"Thanks." He looked bashful for a moment. "I haven't decided if I want to carry the tile through the whole house or not. Plus," he rolled a shoulder, "I'm struggling with paint colors. Gut says to go white, but I just don't want it to look neutral. Mom had the walls all different colors, so it seems like a terrible idea to stick with white walls."

"Paint is something easy to change," I said lightly as I turned back to him. "Go with your favorite colors," I started then thought better of it. "As long as your favorite colors aren't still bright orange and mud brown." I had to remember that sometimes boys didn't make good decisions when it came to decorating schemes.

"I'll remember that," he snorted and led the way back to the living room. "Where's the pizza you were supposed to bring with you?"

"I'll call it in," I promised as I found the least skanky folding chair he had. I got here first, so I had the right to claim it. "I figured I had time." I got comfortable, then looked at him, considering the real reason I'd come early.

Lucas sat beside me, and he didn't look like he'd been ready for company. He wore a tattered white shirt and basketball shorts. The growth of hair on his face was a little thicker, looking more like the start of a beard than peach fuzz. The hair on his head was disheveled, and while the bed looked made, I was wondering if he'd been napping.

"So, what's up, Buttercup?" He raised an eyebrow at me.

"Gonna make me say it, huh?" I sighed as I asked. "We both know you already know."

"Do I need to kick his ass?" His face was serious, and I didn't doubt that he wouldn't.

"No," I snapped. I rubbed my face then instantly regretted it. I had forgotten about the makeup I took the time to put on. I gave my hand a look to see if it was smudged on my hands. "B didn't force himself on me. You know him better than that."

"I know he doesn't like to do what he's told," Lucas grunted back at me, his irritation evident. "He's supposed to keep his hands to himself," he said plainly, like it was law, but I just wasn't in the know.

"Who told him to keep his hands to himself?" I asked even though I knew the answer. I just wanted him to admit it.

He shot me a look, then shook his head. "I did." He rubbed his hands together as if he were considering his words. "It didn't become an issue until you grew out of the scabbed knees and snot nose." He bit his lip and seemed to be searching for something to focus on, refusing to look at me. "Do you have any idea how beautiful you are?"

That caught me off guard. "What?"

"Even when we were all awkward, I could see him mooning after you." His voice went a little harsh as he spoke. He closed his eyes, and I watched his face for any kind of sign that he would crack out a, 'Just kidding.' Only, he wouldn't look at me. "I couldn't let him do something stupid and chase you off. Especially when other boys realized just what you looked like and you weren't as high maintenance as other girls. You see why I would tell 'em to keep their hands to themselves, right?"

That's when he looked at me, his blue eyes desperate. "Them?" I asked. I thought I had a handle on what I was going on here, but here he was, airing it all out.

He made a face at me. "You're gonna make me spell it out?"

"I just need to be clear on it," I said honestly. "I don't want there to be any assumptions and me end up being wrong. I don't want to come out of this looking stupid." I shrugged at him helplessly. "Don't blame me for wanting it obvious."

"I never pegged you for oblivious." He looked resigned as he said it. "Everybody here," he grumbled, "has had a thing for you on more than one occasion. The easiest way I could think to handle it was to not let anybody do anything. You never expressed interest in any of us, so why press the issue? That doesn't make us in the friend zone." He narrowed his eyes at me. "Fucking you... it wouldn't be enough. I can't speak for Noah or Bryce, but I know when I see them look at you, they want more."

My heart kicked up, thumping loud in my ears. It was what I wanted to hear. It confirmed a lot of what I felt, especially considering how Bryce had been around me. Maybe he finally decided to throw caution, and Lucas' words, to the wind.

Right now, it sounded like a good idea.

"Why not press it?" I looked away from him; I was a little afraid of what I might see on his face. I knew rejection wouldn't be there, but the confidence I felt had dwindled away. This wouldn't be a random hook up, or another failed relationship.

These were my boys.

"What if it didn't work out?" He asked like he was reading my thoughts. "What if whoever was with you made the rest of us jealous? Is being selfish worth wrecking it all?"

He was right, and I knew it. But...

I stood up and looked at him. "Sometimes you have to take a chance." His mouth opened like he had an argument ready. Like this was a conversation he either had before, or he had practiced. But I didn't want to hear him crow priorities at me again. So I bent down, and to cut him off, I cupped his face with both hands and got his attention in a way I probably never had before.

I bit the bullet. I closed the distance between us and pressed my lips to his. I tilted my head just slightly, worried about my nose knocking against his. I didn't want it to be awkward. I didn't want to regret this or come away from it with him thinking I was a horrible kisser. I didn't press for more than just a caress, a light taste of his lips without any effort to break the seam of his mouth. The temptation I had felt with Bryce roared into a hunger for Lucas that I wasn't prepared for.

I pulled back when he didn't seem to respond. I expected some sort of rejection, and I stepped back so he could lay it on me gently. Or I hoped gently. The beat of my heart drummed in my ears, and I was suddenly worried.

What if I fucked everything up?

Lucas' face was neutral, which didn't give me any comfort. He stood now that I gave him room to move, and I suddenly expected him to escort me to the door. My breath hitched, and my throat felt tight.

I'm such an idiot.

"Frankie…" His voice was low, and I waited for him to break it to me. He cupped my cheek with one hand, his thumb brushing just under my eye like he saw the tears. Then he hovered over me, invading my space and catching me off guard. I shouldn't have been.

He drifted down to me, catching me mid gasp as he kissed me. He didn't press like Bryce did; it was a cursory exploration. There was the brush of our lips together, then the sweep of his tongue. I felt dizzy at the taste of him. I fisted a hand in his shirt and struggled to remind myself to breathe.

All I thought about before this was a kiss, testing the priorities that Lucas had set for the group. But if a kiss could knock me for a loop like this… I wanted more.

He pulled back a little, and I felt the hurried breath against my face. I didn't open my eyes to see him; I just stood there, hoping he wouldn't pull away. I wanted him to kiss me again so badly. I heard him swallow, and there was a brush of his mouth against mine again. I pressed forward for more.

Then the doorbell rang. That same weird buzz from before, like it was giving a death rattle.

I bit my lip to keep from cursing. I pulled away from Lucas and went to answer it. If this was anything, it was a testament that I should move forward. I shouldn't hold onto the past like Lucas was. We could grow. We were adults.

I opened the door to see Bryce standing there with Noah at his shoulder. When Noah raised a six-pack towards me, I realized what I missed.

"I forgot the fucking pizza," I admitted to them.

"You had one job," Noah complained as he pushed into Lucas' house. "That was the whole selling point at getting us here was pizza and beer." He turned to give Bryce a glare, who had been lingering in the doorway, "C'mon. Let's get this over with."

"I'll order delivery." I had my phone out quickly. "Pepperoni and meat lovers. That should be enough, right?" I shot a look at the three men as I asked.

"Pepperoni? Are we kids?" B shot back at me.

"Gimme a Hawaiian then." I shot him a one-fingered salute and closed the front door, not even giving my old childhood home a second look. I would see Mama on another day off. When I turned to give my attention to my boys, I was faced with looks I couldn't remember ever seeing.

Lucas' eyes were darker than usual. He looked at me with a hunger I felt the echo of. My face grew hot under his gaze, and I turned to eye the other two men. Bryce looked a little petulant, leaving me to guess that Noah had probably been riding him for most of the day. Noah's arms were folded over his chest, and he was a striking image next to the other two casually dressed men in his business suit.

"Can we get the chastising over with?" Bryce demanded. "I did a bad thing." He went on looking from Lucas to Noah. "I don't regret it and given the chance…" He looked at me, and I saw the conviction there. "I'd do it again."

"Yeah well…" Lucas looked back at me. "I was ready to bust you up for it, but somebody objected."

"Did you?" There was hope on Bryce's face when he asked me.

"Why?" Noah, on the other hand, looked irritated, almost jealous. But I didn't want to be arrogant enough to think it might be that.

"Well…" I took a deep breath as I tried to prepare myself for their reactions. "This is why I wanted to talk to all three of you." I fidgeted with my t-shirt and tried to focus on something beyond them, so I wouldn't falter on what I wanted to say. I had their attention, and I felt the weight of their gazes on me. "The priority is and has always been thinking of the group—don't endanger our friendship. I get that; that's important to me too." I took a breath, trying to gather my courage. "But it occurred to me that we all want the same thing."

"What do we all want?" Noah asked, his eyes were narrowed and he looked suspicious. I imagined that this was probably his lawyer face. His lips were a thin line, and his eyebrows were drawn together.

Nerves choked me, and my mouth felt dry. I wouldn't chicken out. I opened my mouth to say, 'Me,' but it seemed like the most arrogant thing to say. I knew they wanted me, but… wasn't there a more tactful way to put it? I'd come here with a damn plan, and I didn't even think about the best way to put it into words.

Good one, Moore. Screw this up and screw everything else up.

"Her," Bryce finished for me. "I mean, after today, I think it's a bit obvious. I've gotten nothing but shit from the both of you." He looked between Noah and Lucas. "Both of you complaining that I'm fucking things up, and I can't keep my hands to myself, when you know you're only riding me because you wished you had the balls to do it. You want her just as much as I do," he snapped at Noah. "You have the same damn problem that I do, and you know it." He laughed a little, running a hand through his hair. "Which is so fucking funny when you think about how you ride me about the women I go through."

That confused me. "Problem?" I piped up. Generally, if there was a problem with one of them, I knew about it.

"You complain about how I treat other women," Bryce directed at me. "I treat them like crap, and they move on when they get sick of me," he said it like a reminder. Then he pointed at Noah. "You don't take them seriously until they get tired of waiting on you to take it to the next level, so they drop you like it's hot." He turned towards Lucas. "They don't even get past the one-night stand with you. And you wanna know why?" He was back to me, Bryce put his hands on his hips like he expected me to answer.

I only floundered. "How am I supposed to know?" I squeaked a little at the end, like I was back to being a teenager.

"I compare every woman who wants my attention to you," Bryce said evenly. "They don't add up." He released a breath then started again, "There's no connection like I feel with you. Other women are just so much more high maintenance that I haven't even attempted for anything more than casual sex."

"So, you're saying I'm the reason you haven't had a good relationship? You're putting that blame on me?" I couldn't fathom that. It seemed ridiculous.

"No," Noah answered for Bryce. "You're not to blame for us wanting someone who feels the same as you," he said gently. "You're suggesting we cross the line. All of us. How does that work?" He tactfully put us back on track.

"Think about what you want? You say you want her?" Lucas spoke up, at last, nodding towards me. "How do you want her? Just for sex?"

"More," Bryce said without hesitation. Noah echoed him. His gaze was on me, and it felt heavy.

"How do we make it work?" Lucas asked, looking at me now.

I stalled out there. "I mean, we keep on as we have been?" I shrugged helplessly. "I mean the only difference between us before and now is that I'm aware of your actual feelings towards me. You don't have to withhold anything from here on."

"There's a little more to it than that." Bryce took a step towards me. "I liked kissing you. I wanted to do more. And I can tell you it would be the same way for these assholes." He gestured to the other men. "The ideal," he said as he closed the distance between us, "is for our friendship to stay the way it is and do that."

The closer Bryce got to me, the more obvious it was what he wanted. I didn't back away when he invaded my space; I let him drift down to kiss me. It wasn't unlike the kiss he gave me that morning, he just put more behind it this time. There wasn't anything tentative about the way he swept his tongue into my mouth, but there was a reminder of the want I felt this morning.

I didn't pull away, and I didn't fight him. I let him kiss me in front of our two best friends, and I didn't think outside the smell of him. Outside his taste. I didn't realize he was moving me or moving closer until I felt my back against the wall. Then, as a noise drifted to my ears, I felt the length of Bryce against me. There was a height difference, something I'd been keenly aware of growing up, but now he stooped over me and pressed every bit of muscle against me.

I take back every time I'd ever called him chunky. There was nothing soft about him now. Especially not what was sandwiched between us. Feeling his erection against me only seemed to throw gasoline on what had been a slow burn with Lucas.

His hand stayed close to my face for the most part, but I wanted to do more. I fisted my hands in his shirt and tugged it up. I wanted to touch skin. It was like an inexplicable need that suddenly occurred to me.

Maybe it was the stress of adjusting to a new work schedule, maybe it was the fact the last time I'd had sex was with Kenny the day before I decided I couldn't give up my friends for him.

How long ago was that? A week ago? More than that?

My fingers touched skin, and Bryce groaned against my mouth. I echoed the noise, and that's when I realized I'd been making little sounds from the moment he kissed me. It was like a sign, this was the right route to take. I needed this, and if Bryce's reaction was anything, it was just an echo of my own desires.

Desires that Noah and Lucas felt, too.

A throat cleared, and Bryce slowly pulled away from me. "It's hard not to get carried away," he said softly, his voice so deep it did things to me. I clenched my thighs together, and I glanced at Noah, feeling almost drunk with want.

It didn't matter that he'd been watching me to kiss Bryce. It should've mattered, but right at that moment, I didn't care. Noah was just at Bryce's shoulder, and his eyes were so dilated, they looked black.

"This is a test, isn't it?" Noah asked, his voice at a low husk like Bryce's. "To see if I'm gonna get pissed and clock you one?"

"If you're going to, you might as well do it now." Bryce rolled a shoulder as he said it. "As long as you don't punch me in the dick, we'll be okay. That'd be more than just a low blow." As he spoke, he made a pointed adjustment to his obvious erection.

Noah seemed to focus on me, taking up the space Bryce had vacated. His hands cupped my face, and he forced me to meet him halfway, catching my lips and kissing me. The kiss started out hungry, throwing more fuel onto the already roaring flames that had built inside me. Then he slowed, as if he were suddenly basking in the taste, and it made everything intensify. He had a scent richer than Bryce's. The cologne he wore was musky, and I drowned in the smell of him as much as I was his flavor. There was a distinct difference between the flavors of the two men, but strangely enough, I wasn't put off by it at all.

When he pulled away, I didn't resist the urge to follow him. I kissed him hungrily; you don't start a fire like this and try to walk away from it. I wrapped an arm around his shoulders and dug a hand into his hair like I could keep him from pulling away. He didn't try; he pressed me back against the wall and groaned. I didn't think, but it was like we tapped into something, and I wasn't ready to pull away from it.

Had Kenny been right? Were you able to want someone without realizing it? It felt like there'd been something pent up when I kissed Lucas, and I felt it echoed with Bryce and Noah.

I could let go and let this happen without regret.

A buzzing cut through the haze. I didn't pull away from Noah, but I heard Lucas say, "You need to stop unless you want to give the pizza guy an eyeful." He didn't sound angry.

I needed to come up for air. I was dizzy when I looked at him, confused.

"Pizza?" I gasped.

"Damn," Noah moaned as he pried himself away from me. He put a hand against the wall and took a deep breath. "If we do anything like that here, we're gonna have to get this asshole some damn curtains."

I took a glance out the window. It was positioned close enough to the door that I could see the pizza man there. He looked pointedly at the ground. "Shit." I fished my wallet from my pocket and opened the front door. I felt the heat creeping up my neck, and I tried my best to feign indifference when I looked at the stranger on Lucas' front porch. "How much do I owe you?"

"Twenty-two fifty," the pizza guy offered. "You guys having a party?" He eyed me, and I couldn't tell if he was asking to join or not.

"Not that kind of party," B said, taking the pizzas from him.

I handed him two twenties without caring about the change. "Keep it," I said, before I closed the front door and leaned against it. "Blinds, he needs blinds with blackout curtains." I covered my face with my hands. "I wasn't thinking. If Mama happened to look this way, she could've seen something."

"If she did, she'd probably beat down the door," Noah assured me, taking my hand from my face. He led me to the chairs Lucas had set out for us.

"She's gonna think I'm a sex-fueled heathen." I didn't bother hiding my worry. "She always thought you guys would be a negative influence on me." I sat heavily in one chair. The plastic creaked ominously, and I leaned onto my knees.

"You got pineapples on this pizza." B made a disgusted noise as he opened the top pizza box. "You are a heathen." He tossed the box onto the floor in front of me. "What kind of monster does that?"

Something about the easy banter he reverted to took the stress right out of me. I looked from Bryce to Lucas. "We can make this work?" I didn't mean for it to come out as a question, but I felt like I needed to look at him for validation.

He sat next to me, reaching down to pluck a slice from the box on the floor. "We'll figure it out." He sounded reassuring. "In the meantime, we'll have to figure out how we're gonna do this with your schedule."

"The same way we did things before," Bryce said around a mouthful. "Just now instead of hanging out, there might be sex." He smirked back at me like he expected me to argue.

"The only reason sex isn't happening now is because dude," I nodded towards Lucas, "doesn't have anything covering the windows." I didn't feel bad about admitting that. My blood was still pounding. The only thing keeping me behaved was the idea that Mama would just look this way and see it.

"It's on the to-do list," Lucas grumbled.

8

It'd been about two weeks after it had been decided that we'd cross the line that Lucas had drawn for us. We just... we just hadn't actually crossed the line. It was a mutual decision between the four of us. I just wished I'd taken into account that I had no real free time.

My boys understood; no one pressed for more now that we had agreed that more could happen. I just hated that I was on an overnight shift now, and anytime I wasn't working, I was sleeping. It just added more time to the dry spell I'd been on, and I felt a growing ache that pulsed within me.

It was just a shame that I was so tired when I walked out of Mercy to find Noah waiting on the curb. I couldn't give him more than a zombified grunt. He leaned against a black sedan. It looked new, a sporty coupe. It surprised me. Mrs. Kemp was always frugal, and growing up, they didn't buy new cars. They would ride around in beaters until the beaters died.

He had a coffee cup in hand and a nervous smile on his face. "Hey there, doc." He offered me the cup.

"Counselor." I smiled tiredly at him. "I was just going home to pass out." I took the cup and pried off the top, a milky brown liquid greeted me. I took a sip without further question and groaned at the sweetness. "Chocolate latte. You're the best."

"I try." He stepped away from the car to open the door. "Care for a ride home?"

I considered it, sipping the latte greedily. "What are the chances you could take me to your place?"

He paused at the door, holding it open for me. "It wasn't what I came here for, but I'm not dumb enough to say no to that." He tilted his head a little as he looked at me. "I just thought I'd take a page from Bryce's book. Knowing that you're busting ass, I figured I'd pay my bestie a visit."

I snorted into the cup and stepped down to sit in his car. I entertained myself with the warm liquid. If there was a coffee God, I'd be praying to him now. I hummed as I slurped it down, not paying attention as he sat next to me.

"Girl," he made a noise, "if I knew it was that easy to get sexy sounds out of you, I would have brought you coffee a long time ago."

"Work a twelver," I mumbled around the lip of a cup. "Be a nurse's bitch for the majority of it. You'll groan sexily into a cup of coffee, too."

"You're a nurse's bitch?" He started the car and got us rolling. "Is that in a sexy way? Because I can get behind that."

I snorted and shook my head. "She rides me, but in an unfun way." I rolled a shoulder and put the cup into the console so I could give him a curious look. "I'm not gonna complain. I figure she's putting me on the right route to make sure I don't kill anyone."

"A lot more high-pressure stuff than I could deal with," he commented lightly, driving with his full focus on the road.

I shifted further into the seat, realizing that they were leather. I whistled. "This is a new car. When did you get this?" I gave him a harder look. He wasn't dressed in the suits he worked in, but he had on dark-gray slacks and a light-blue button down that complemented his darker skin tone. He was dressed like he was trying to impress.

I felt flattered suddenly.

"I got it after my first paycheck." He laughed a little. "I was so used to Mom's grocery go-getters that I felt like I needed to splurge. She was pissed, too, you know?" His expression sobered as he kept his eyes on the road. "I just felt like I earned it."

"Take it from me," I started evenly. "After all the education and grinding information into your skull, the first real paycheck is something to be proud of. You earned this." I patted the console between us. "It's nice. I can't say that this would be my first major purchase, but I see the appeal."

"What's your first major purchase gonna be?" he asked as he pulled into the parking lot of what looked like an upscale apartment complex. It was a definite step up from the apartment I shared with Sara.

"I haven't decided. There's this big temptation to get my own place," I admitted as I rubbed a hand over my face. After this long-ass day, caffeine wouldn't keep me going for too long. "But I feel like I should save it. I can't live off Mom and Dad forever either." I grimaced because I had come to an impasse.

"You got options," he said offhandedly.

I hummed but didn't poke him to elaborate on it. I was too tired for that kind of conversation. He led the way into a classy-looking lobby. It had marble floors with oriental rugs and wood grain that somehow managed to not date the place. He led me to an elevator and took me to the second floor. The hallway we stepped out onto was similar to the lobby, with marble floors but white walls, likely so it would appear brighter with the lack of windows. There were also four slate-blue doors with brass numbers on each.

Noah stopped at the first one on the left. He had his keys in hand and didn't pay much attention to me until he had the door open. Then I had his full attention as he directed me into his apartment. This was the first time I'd been here, not that Noah hadn't ever offered his place for our gatherings, But if they ever happened, it wasn't something I'd been a part of. It always seemed natural to go back to Lucas', likely because he still lived in our old stomping ground.

Noah's apartment had darker wood floors, and the walls were a stark white. He had it sparsely decorated, with a sofa in front of a large television sitting on a simple entertainment center. Exactly what I expected of him, all my boys really.

They kept things simple.

I didn't wait for him to offer to give me a tour, I took the initiative to walk through the broad, open layout. The front door opened directly into his living room, which was attached to a kitchen. I saw what looked like granite and stainless steel appliances. At a glance, it looked clean. I was willing to bet it was barely used.

"If you want some breakfast, I can scramble some eggs," Noah offered from behind me. "I think I might have some bacon."

"I'm good," I assured him as I opened doors. I found a pantry half full of easy meals. A lot of macaroni and cheese boxes. I snickered without giving him a second look. "You know how to cook?"

"The basics." When I did look at him, he had a hand on his neck, and he looked mildly embarrassed. I hadn't seen it on him before. But the darkening on his cheeks suited him.

Why hadn't I seen that on him before?

I went out on a further investigation, finding his laundry room and finally his bedroom. A large, unmade bed took up most of the room, and there was a dresser at the other end next to a door that was either a closet or a bathroom. I lingered in the doorway, tempted in the wrong way by his bed. I could see myself curling up in it and falling asleep.

"I can take you home," he offered. It gave me a clue as to how close he was. "I didn't take into consideration that I was depriving you of sleep." I felt his hand brush against the length of my back. "I just wanted to see you while I had a chance."

I turned towards him and said, "No. I'd make more time if I had it." I considered him; there was a certain nervousness to the set of his shoulders. Did I do that? I leaned against the door frame, looking at him. "You have a chance anytime you want," I offered. My fatigue gave me a certain bravado I normally wouldn't have.

The distance between us dwindled, and his pupils dilated noticeably. "I want a chance," he murmured. His voice was low and made things in me knot up.

I put a hand on his chest, fingering the light-blue linen. But his eyes held me, the dark-brown almost black now. It drew me in, and I pressed a chaste kiss against his lips, but it was more like pressing a button. One of his arms came around me and pulled me flush against him. His other hand tangled up in my hair, loosening the tie that held my hair in a ponytail. He gave my hair a tug until I followed his direction. Then his mouth slanted against mine, his tongue probing my lips apart so he could swirl his tongue against my own.

There was a mixture of breath, a groan I couldn't tell who made, and a gasp I knew came from me. I slid my arms around his shoulders, and it felt good to touch him. He didn't give much space to pull away; he seemed too intent on kissing me, but he let me part long enough for a breath.

It was almost overwhelming. There was fatigue on top of the lust coming off him in waves.

But much like that night at Lucas', kissing him ignited something in me that left me wanting more. My hands drifted along the length of Noah's broad shoulders, and I wound them down his chest until I came across buttons. After a little fumbling, I followed that line until I met the braided leather of his belt. I hesitated there.

Talk was one thing. Kissing them was another. But doing more would mean no going back.

The hand in my hair tightened, and I heard the whimper coming from me. He pulled away then. I heard him panting, but I couldn't tell if he was on the same train of thought as I was. His grip on my hair loosened, and his hand drifted down to cup my face. "Second thoughts?" His lips brushed against mine gently, and I opened my eyes to meet his. I could see the nervousness looking back at me.

I felt the echo of it.

"No going back after this," I answered truthfully. "Not just from us," I continued.

He nodded and started to pull away from me. I realized then that I didn't want him to. My fingers slipped past the belt and into the soft linen of his slacks. I felt hot skin, and I saw something on his face twitch. "I don't want to go back," he murmured.

I tugged at the waist of his slacks before I decided to loosen the clasp of his belt. As soon as I had his belt open, I had the button and zipper down. I shoved his slacks down and took control of the situation.

"Me either," I whispered before I went in for another kiss.

He stood before me in just his underwear. I didn't take the time to see what my friend preferred, boxers or briefs. I traced my hands along the bare skin. I made my way up his back, tracing lines and feeling every reaction he had to me. I felt the growing erection against my hip and the little shivers he made as my fingernails traced over his skin.

Noah's hands worked as I took advantage of his near nakedness. He tugged my scrub top from my pants and delved underneath. His hand drifted up to cup one breast through my bra. The other hand shoved past the elastic of the pants and cupped my ass, pressing my hips flush against his.

As much as I wanted this, I didn't want to stay up against the doorjamb. I tugged away from him, drawing out a noise from him that I found I liked. I pushed his hand from my top and pulled the other from my pants. When I met his gaze, I saw confusion and a little bit of fear. To soothe his addled nerves, I tried to give him my sexiest smile. I didn't wait to see if it would have the desired effect. Instead, I decided to even out the playing field.

I had the rough synthetic material of my scrub top up and over my head before he could close the distance between us again. His attention went to the most obvious place after that. With his eyes now on my chest, I took the time to kick off my shoes and wiggle out of the scrub pants. I didn't want to wait for him to take me to his bed. I needed to get off my aching feet. Without giving him a further look, I went the rest of the way into his bedroom and flopped onto his bed.

Probably not my sexiest move, but at this point, I didn't care. If he wanted me bad enough, he'd overlook it.

I propped myself up on my elbows and sighed at him. "I don't have the energy in my arsenal to be a sex kitten."

"I could just let you sleep." He looked relaxed. A quick glance down at the tent in his boxers told me it was an offer he hoped I wouldn't take him up on.

"If I try to sleep now, I'm gonna regret it to the point that I won't be able to sleep." I reached out with my foot to brush my toes up his thigh. "So, we can forge ahead with this, and you can make sure I crash hard."

"That a challenge?" He grabbed my ankle before I could get close to the tent of his boxers. "I remember telling you about how it's supposed to be done." I raised an eyebrow at that. "Now you're giving me the opportunity to show you." He went down to his knees, getting my attention in a way that had everything standing at attention. "So," he set my ankle onto his shoulder, "I'm gonna say challenge accepted."

I opened my mouth to protest; I wasn't keen on oral sex. I hadn't had an experience where it worked out in a pleasurable way. It always seemed awkward, and I was usually twisting my fingers, waiting for the guy between my legs to decide he was finished tonguing my labia.

Noah's eyes connected with mine, and it was like he seized my apprehension. He brushed his cheek against my calf, then slowly followed the length of my leg, with his cheek rubbing against my skin. The heat flared, and it was like he lit a path of fire up my leg. He didn't have any stubble that I could see, but I felt roughness as he pressed against the back of my knee, like he tightened a thread that led all the way up to the throbbing nerves between my thighs.

Anticipation was what I was feeling.

Maybe it was never good before because I didn't want the person I was with half as much as I wanted Noah. I felt it in the thrum of my heart and the way my blood seemed to heat every inch of my skin just from the fathomless look in his eyes as his tongue swept out across the skin of my thigh. He left a trail of goosebumps, and I took a deep breath as he got to the junction of skin where my thigh met my hip. He didn't push past the elastic barrier of my panties, and a choked noise came out of me. He huffed out a laugh, and I clenched the muscles within me.

"Please." The word hissed out of me without my control. Like my body knew what it wanted, and it wasn't above taking control to ask for it.

His fingers pushed aside my silky panties, and I felt the puff of his breath against me. I had enough thought to wish I'd shaved, or that I'd groomed in some way other than the lazy routine I'd taken up since I started my residency. But I saw nothing on his face that showed repulsion.

He nuzzled against my exposed lips, and my breath caught again. I felt my heart quicken, and if it had beat any harder, it would have drowned out any noise I made. Well, until he swept his tongue along the part of my lips over the line of my slit. I choked again, and my head fell back against his bed when he parted my lips. He tilted his head so he could tease my opening better with his tongue.

My legs twitched, and for some reason, I felt the need to close them... Especially when he found the throbbing bundle of nerves at the top of my opening. He shouldered both my legs, keeping me from edging him out. There was a little struggle, me rolling my hips against his face and him wrapping his arms around my pelvis to hold me still. Then I felt teeth against me. There was a light pinch, and my eyes shot open. I looked down at him and saw the challenge in his eyes. He lashed my clit with his tongue, working it in a way that gave me no time to adjust.

My head fell back, and I arched my back, trying for relief and to compensate for the fact that it rushed through me like fire eating through dry timber. I felt his hand reach under me and flick loose the hooks of my bra before he shoved it upward. If the room was cool, I didn't feel it, but my nipples were already stiffened without the stimulation.

He sucked my clit into his mouth just as he cupped a breast, twisting his fingers around the stiff nipple until it bordered on painful. I heard the noise I made echoed through the room, and I felt his answering groan against me.

"Oh God. Do that again," came out of me in a rushed breath.

He groaned. It was long, and it vibrated through me so deliciously, the only thing keeping me from spontaneously combusting was just the emptiness in me. But I was so close. I felt it burning in my fingertips and toes.

Then his mouth left me.

I whined and started to sit up so I could make a complaint, but the hand on my breast pressed me back down. Then I felt him shove a finger into me, and it curled upward to the point that I didn't care that he wasn't seducing me with his mouth and tongue.

"I remember..." His voice was a low growl. "I remember telling you how this was supposed to be." I felt him place a wet kiss against my thigh. "You feel that?" He brushed his chin against my skin, and I felt the dampness he spread. "You are this wet because of me. You realize that, right?" His fingers started to withdraw only to work their way back in. "You're this wet for me."

"Yes," I hissed out because there was no arguing with him. Not when he had me right where I was about to be blown apart.

"Say it," he barked at me. "Say it, Frankie."

"I'm wet," I managed. "For you."

Then his mouth was back on me, and the hand in me worked in tandem with his tongue. I made another strangled noise, and my hands fisted in the comforter beneath me as I tried to keep myself from burning up. But there was no stopping it.

I didn't recognize the noises I made. I was too caught up in blowing to pieces, and it was like I was scattered on the wind like ash. My nerves buzzed, and everything was a humming mess of limbs and organs I couldn't keep track of.

Or maybe that humming was coming from Noah. He pulled his fingers from me and swept his tongue along my tender bits like he was savoring the taste of a good meal. I shuddered hard with each pull he took. He'd devoured me.

I didn't feel anything outside of that residual burn, and the warmth that lingered still in my belly. My nerve endings were still buzzing on a high I couldn't recall ever being on before. I didn't pay him much attention... not very courteous or grateful, I know.

I heard a drawer open somewhere in the room, then I felt his weight on the mattress. I slit my eyes open to look at him through my eyelashes. It was almost like I was drunk. I was ready to just lie back and let him have his way.

He didn't dive right in like I would have expected him to. "Are you gonna fall asleep on me now?" His voice sounded deeper than usual, and while the burn had died down to something more residual, the effect his voice felt like it was stoked.

"I should return the favor," I murmured.

"I'm pretty sure at this point if I let you, I'd end up busting before the real fun started." He cupped my face, and I felt dampness against one cheek. I inhaled, and there was a muskiness with it. That was me. That was my scent. "I've had dreams of fucking you for so long, I'm not about to miss this opportunity." His thumb brushed along my bottom lip.

"There'll be other chances to get head," I grinned. "Especially if you give head like that."

"My skills have made it hard to break up with a lot of women," he said as he gave his eyebrows a little waggle. "I've got some motivation to make an impression," he admitted while looking self-conscious suddenly. "You're not gonna fall asleep on me?"

"I think at this point," I sat up so I could get into his face, "you're gonna have to try harder to get me to fall asleep on you."

"Pretty sure I've shown you I'm up for that challenge," he said, his gaze drifting down from my eyes, to my lips, then back again. "Pretty positive the last ten-plus years I've shown you that I've got you handled in all the other aspects."

"Handled?" I laughed a little, tempted to call him on it. But he kissed me like he knew I had an argument ready. I didn't though. There wasn't a real reason to stop this. I was still buzzed and knew that if he had been trying to make an impression with his tongue and fingers, sex wasn't likely to let me down either.

I didn't wait for him to tease me further. As he hovered over me and gave me a taste of myself on his lips and tongue, I reached between us and found his hardened length. I felt the plastic of a condom, and I was impressed. I gave him a few hard strokes without upsetting the barrier he wore.

The groan that came from him was enticing. I wanted to hear more noise from him, and at this moment, there was only one way to do that. I directed him to my entrance and felt him tremble above me before he pressed me back against the bed, and his hips gave a gentle roll forward.

My breath caught as he stretched me. I hadn't paid much attention to his erection, aside from the growing hardness I felt before, but he had a good girth to him, and I hadn't considered how he would feel in me. I clenched my eyes closed when it felt like he had me at the brink, then I felt his hand on my face again.

"Look at me." The demand came out in a harsh whisper. I opened my eyes to see the strain in his eyes, like he was barely holding it together. "Stay with me, Frankie."

I tried to focus on his eyes, but it was a struggle. Especially when he was fully sheathed within me. I could see it, what he was after. I felt it, not just how he stretched me to a fullness I hadn't experienced before, but something in my chest knotted up. I wrapped my arms around his middle, needing to hang on to him.

My legs had been hanging off the bed since I'd flopped onto it. Now, I arched up to wrap them around his hips. It changed the angle of him inside me only slightly, but it felt as if he were in me deeper. The breath hissed out of me, and I heard his catch in response.

"Stay with me," he gritted out.

I felt him withdraw, and my legs reflexively tightened around him so he couldn't pull out too much. It didn't keep him from putting a bit of force behind his thrust once he worked his way back into me. It was a struggle to keep our eyes connected, but I managed. As he built up a rhythm, I didn't let myself falter. I was being pulled tighter with each movement, and it was so hard not to give in to just feel it all.

Noah pushed himself up with his hands, angling away from me. He edged us up further on his bed and predictably, his eyes dropped from mine. It didn't take a rocket scientist to figure out what it was that he was looking at, especially when I moved a hand to catch one of my bouncing breasts.

I took that as an opportunity to stop struggling and to instead maintain focus. I let my attention drift away to the feeling of his cock in me, where we were physically connected and the sparks exploding outward from there. Now that I didn't have him to hold onto, I was stuck fisting the comforter again.

The challenge was to exhaust me to the point I would pass out after this. With the way he rocked into me, using a force that made me see stars, I was sure he was determined to do just that. He was still striving to make an impression. I had enough wherewithal to wonder if he thought that I would regret doing this if he didn't actually fuck my brains out.

I reached down to touch him, just at his pubic bone. He stuttered to a stop, his eyes wide when they shot up to connect with mine. I saw confusion with a shot of fear.

"I'm not going anywhere," I managed to say even though I felt like I was throbbing at the precipice of blowing to pieces again. "I'm staying right here with you," I reiterated.

His brows shot upward, and it looked like he wasn't quite putting it together. So, I sat up and wrapped my arms around his middle. "I'm staying." I pressed my lips against the line between his pectorals.

I felt it when his breath caught. His arms went around me, and he hugged me tightly. "Frank!" Emotion choked the words out of him. I looked up to see a glassiness in his eyes.

"I'm not going anywhere," I assured him again as I reached up to kiss him.

Before our kisses had been hurried, rushed, and in the moment. With this kiss, everything seemed to slow down. He wasn't in a hurry anymore, and while there wasn't any lack of passion by any means, it just added to it.

Especially when his hips moved again.

The closeness, the connection he'd been striving for when he first entered me seemed to take a hold of me now. I didn't let him do all the work. I rolled my hips to move with him, adding to the explosive feeling burning within me. The angle was off, even with him stooping to thrust into me. My moans must have turned into grunts, because without edging out any sort of separation, he pushed us sideways back to lying on his bed.

He maneuvered us a little bit, flexing muscles to get my legs loose from around his hips. He kept us close and held one leg over my hip. He had it so he was able to thrust into me while we were both on our sides. He went deeper, drawing every noise from me into his mouth and echoing it back to me.

That was about when he lost pace with his thrusts. He broke the kiss with a gasp and pressed his brow against mine. He dropped the leg he'd been holding, and I felt his hand wedge between us. He made a desperate noise, and he brushed his fingers back and forth against me, forcing me closer and closer to that edge.

"I can't," he gritted out as his fingers swiped faster. Desperation was a tremor I felt in him as his thrusts stuttered. "You gotta come, Frankie."

"Let go," I managed to choke out. "I'm close." Just not as close as he was.

The fingers on my clit stiffened, and he afforded me a series of rough thrusts before he released a long groan. He melted against me then, leaning half on me. I felt his cock throbbing in me, and I echoed it, hovering on the edge of my own orgasm.

I whimpered, clenching around his softening cock in an attempt to get a little closer to relief. He didn't respond immediately. His eyes were closed, with his forehead pressed against mine. I took it as him still basking in that orgasmic feeling.

I decided that I'd let him have the moment. I covered his hand with mine and slipped his fingers out of the way, so I could tease myself to completion. I don't know if it was because I made a noise or if my inner muscles squeezed him, but somehow I got his attention. He took over for me.

I closed my eyes as he growled at me, getting my attention. "Look at me," he barked out the demand. "Let me see you come."

His hips shifted a little bit, even though his cock wasn't stiff like it had been before. It helped, but what had me teetering was the look in his eyes as his fingers worked me. I couldn't falter this time. It was like he had a hold on me, and I couldn't look away from the dark depths of his eyes.

When he finally pushed me over the edge, the burn wasn't the same as before. I didn't fly to pieces, but I melted like he had sparked lava within me. It was just as good, though I felt more incoherent than I had before.

His fingers brushed against me a final time before he wrapped his arms around me. I struggled to stay awake, but bliss and exhaustion kept weighing me down. Every touch he gave me was just a quiet buzz that added to it.

"This is gonna have to happen again. Once isn't gonna be enough for me," he whispered. "There's no going back from here."

I only managed a hum of agreement as I readily dropped off into darkness.

9

As great as it was to wake up in Noah's bed, his mattress was so much better than mine, and I slept like a baby. I didn't think about the pitfalls of what could happen with me not going home. I didn't have a change of clothes or any of my toiletries. But at some point, after I passed out, Noah had done laundry and had everything I needed before it was time for me to go back to the grind.

It felt like he was trying to take care of me.

It made me realize, looking back, that's what they did. My boys. It was something they'd been doing since I moved into the neighborhood. I liked to think that I had their backs like they had mine. But I wondered if I had anything I could offer them outside of just sex.

It was a crisis I didn't have time for.

Especially when I finally made it home after my shift. Sara was waiting for me in the living room. She had her *New Housewives* on and a bowl of my popcorn in her lap. How'd I know it was mine? Because I always bought it, and she always ate it without buying more. An irksome trait, but I somehow ended up being the bad roommate for the occasional drunken fumbling with keys.

"Where have you been?" she asked around a mouthful of popcorn, not at all put off by the fact she was eating my food. "Did you sleep at the hospital?"

I considered leaving it at that, letting her believe I slept at the hospital because I was too tired. But my mouth got ahead of my brain. "Noah picked me up. I stayed with him," I grunted as I made my way back towards my bedroom.

"Noah?" she echoed after me. "Which one of your men is that now? The tan one? Or was that the one that kissed you?"

I stilled, but I didn't look back at her. I didn't realize she'd kept track of the boys. I couldn't recall the last time Noah had been to the apartment. Had I introduced them? I couldn't remember, I was running on fumes. I rubbed my face and mumbled a 'yeah' back at her before stumbling into my room.

I crashed onto my bed and was out like a light. Still in my scrubs, still in my bra, and still with my shoes on. At this point, I didn't care as long as I could sleep.

***

Blink 182 blared to life, dragging me up from my exhaustion-induced coma. The lyrics 'What's my age again? What's my age again?' played on repeat. It took me a minute to figure out how or why that particular chorus was playing before I realized it was the ringtone I'd set for Bryce. The ringing eventually stopped, and I didn't bother to open my eyes.

Hopefully, he'd figure out that I was asleep and just give up.

The song blared to life again, and this time the light of my phone found a way to drill into my eyes. I didn't even remember pulling it out of my pocket, but there it was, sitting on my bedside table, plugged in. My room was dark save for the brightly lit screen of my phone, even after the call went to voicemail. I watched, with some growing irritation, as the light steadily dimmed, only for it to brighten right back up as it rang again.

"I'm gonna choke 'im," I snarled aloud as I picked up the phone. "You must have a death wish," I said as I answered the call.

"Sleeping Beauty," he greeted me. "You can't just sleep the day away. I just got Lucas to clean himself up so we could go to dinner. Wake your ass up and get ready. I know you got tomorrow off."

It'd been a day since my evening—or was it morning—with Noah. I suppose I shouldn't be surprised. This was what happened when you confided everything in your group of friends and then suddenly you started sleeping together.

"So…" I rubbed my eyes. "He told you."

"What?" He laughed a little bit, telling me just how nervous he was. "What are you talking about?"

"Cut the bullshit." I rolled over onto my back and sighed. "Are you just trying to set up dinner so we can all eventually end up fucking?"

He was quiet for a beat, and it sounded like he was closing a door. "While I wouldn't say no to that, that wasn't the ulterior motive." It sounded like he was carefully choosing his words. "Sex with you…" He paused then cleared his throat. "It wouldn't be just sex. We agreed to that. Noah owned up to what he did, you're right. He told the both of us how he brought you home, and you were completely exhausted… but you gave in."

"And you want me to give in to you, too?" I asked, not resisting the urge to sound angry. It was so Bryce to do this.

"Honestly?" His voice sounded easy, but I could hear a little thread to it. "Yeah. I want you just as much as Noah does," he said. He, also, said does. Not did. I sat up, cradling the phone to my ear. "I can tell you without a doubt that Lucas is on the same bandwagon as we are. But you knew that. We came clean about that."

"And you expect me to fuck you tonight then? You take me to dinner, and then I put out?" I shot back at him with a wave of anger I didn't get at first. The more I spoke and thought about it, the more pressure I felt. "I slept with Noah because I wanted to. At the time, I didn't consider how it would affect the group, but that doesn't mean I have to immediately get in your pants."

"Frank," he snapped at me. "That is not what I'm saying."

"Then what are you saying?" I tried not to sound exasperated, but I couldn't help it.

"Dinner," he grumped into the phone. "It'll be me and Lucas. Do you think he's gonna let me be well…" Bryce stalled at that. I heard him take a breath, "He's not gonna let me be me." He had a good point there. "Just…" He made a disgruntled noise. "Just let me take you out for dinner. We can make it a group thing like usual."

I had a final moment where I considered hanging up on him. "I'm up. You have to stop waking me up." I heard the whine in my voice, and I grimaced in response. It wasn't something I liked to do, and I was sure I'd get grief for it.

"Can't stay in bed all day, chump. Get up." He hung up on me then.

I flopped back in my bed and groaned at the lost chance at getting caught up on sleep. I didn't afford myself too long to pout though. I knew if I did, Bryce would probably barge in to drag me out of bed. So, I got up and took my time getting ready, not because I wanted to make an impression. These guys had seen me at my worst; there was no real reason to candy coat myself when they knew what I looked like snot nosed and without makeup.

I was putting an earring in as I walked out of my bedroom and nearly dropped it. Lucas was on his phone on the couch, and Bryce was in the kitchen with Sara. Ugh. There was nothing good that could come from that, and I could only grimace at my friend as he chatted with my roommate.

"I didn't realize you guys were already here," I said before sinking down onto the couch next to Lucas. "What's up, Buttercup?"

"Our party of four is up to five," he grunted at me without looking up from his phone. "Noah's gonna meet us at the restaurant," he reported. He took a moment to rub his hand through the growth on his face. "I don't know what the plan was for tonight. If he had one."

"You heard the conversation?" I asked, suddenly unsure how I came off while speaking my fears to Bryce. I said things to him I wouldn't have said to Lucas.

"Half of it." He looked at me then. "You think he's waiting for his turn?"

I nodded. I didn't want to voice my answer to him. Or my fears, not with Sara in earshot. Bryce, on the other hand, would hear my concerns or figure them out on his own. I wouldn't get any judgments from him.

"He is." Lucas gave the kitchen a look as he said it, his voice low. "So am I. Just like Noah is waiting for another turn."

So, it was just sex then? I leaned away from Lucas for a moment. Now all I wanted to do was go back to bed. This wasn't something I wanted to hear.

"Something you've got to take into consideration..." H leaned close so he could whisper, "This comes from years of wanting you. Years of loving you. And you said yourself you wanted to cross that line." I looked at him then, feeling something twist up inside me as I got lost in his gaze. "This is something you have to face when you cross that line."

"It's not just sex?" I asked in a whisper.

Lucas snorted and rolled his eyes. "No."

I wanted to ask more, but I heard Sara's laugh before she came into the living room. Lucas' expression was like a mirror of what I felt. There was no love loss for Sara; she was my roommate, so she was tolerated by my friends. But her behavior had been off-putting; she flirted with each of my guys without any care to whom she was directing her attempts.

At least none of them had been receptive.

"Noah's got us a table at Vine," B said. His shoulders had a tight set to them, and the way Sara invaded his personal space might've had something to do with it. He gave me a pleading look as he headed towards the door. "We're all gonna pile into my car."

"I call shotgun." Sara grinned at me before heading out the front door after him. "Lock up, Fran," she said over a shoulder like it was an afterthought.

"I think this is the first time she's actually wormed her way into a night out with us," I said to Lucas as we followed. I took the time to flick off the light switches in the kitchen and living room. Lucas waited out on the step with me as I locked the door. "What'd she say to get an invite?"

"She said, 'Where we going?' to Bryce and invited herself." He rolled his shoulders and ran a hand through his hair. "Neither of us were thrilled by the idea. We were hoping to be able to talk about where we go from here. I think we have the understanding that she doesn't need to know what we're doing." He walked with me to Bryce's rumbling car in the parking lot; it was a remake of the older model muscle cars.

Cars weren't something I ever cared about; they were just useful to get from point A to point B. I was perfectly fine with walking or using public transportation. But boys and their toys.

"Yeah, she's been calling me greedy since I moved in, and she saw you guys." We paused outside of the car as I spoke. I thought it was a good opportunity for a private conversation. "I can't imagine what she'd say if she found out she was right."

"Or told your mom for that matter." Lucas smiled a little at that. Damn was he right. I could only imagine the conniption fit she would have if she knew I'd been intimate with Noah. I was fairly sure she thought I was still a virgin.

He opened the back-passenger door for me, something he'd done a half-dozen times before. I never thought anything of it. Now it left me questioning if there were any other obvious signs that they cared for me more than I thought. Lucas trotted around the back of the car to slide in next to me. I'd been so distracted by the gesture that I hadn't paid attention to the other two people in the car.

When I looked up, I met Bryce's gaze. I had his undivided attention, despite Sara's efforts to get his. Would jealousy be an issue? I didn't know what to do at this moment. The smile I forced probably was just as awkward as I felt. It made the car ride extra uncomfortable, especially when I noticed Sara putting her hand on top of Bryce's where it rested on the gear shift. If there was any question of what he wanted, it became evident when he pulled his hand from under hers and rested it on the steering wheel.

I shouldn't have been satisfied with that. I shouldn't have enjoyed it. But I smiled anyway and pointedly looked at the rearview mirror. When he noticed me, I got a wink in return.

It was a relief to know that I was in some good standing with two out of my three boys. I just wish our uninvited guest wasn't putting a damper on the evening. The car ride was quiet with Sara's poor attempts to draw out a conversation with B. She fangirled about his stilted college career, something that ended in an injury he hadn't been able to bounce back from. Something I knew was a sore subject with him.

It made sense that he picked up a career in physical therapy. It also made sense why he went through women the way he did. If I hadn't lived with her, it was likely Sara would've been just another conquest—that's what she wanted from him.

Introspective thoughts about B made me miss the fact that we pulled to a stop in a parking lot. The opening of car doors brought me back to reality, and I had mine open before Lucas could get around the car. He was still there to offer me a hand as I got out. The warmth I got from it gave me a reason to toss aside my grievances and worries altogether. Whatever happened tonight, I would appreciate my friends.

Just in a new way.

We were almost to the restaurant door when someone realized there was only three of us. A hand swatted my shoulder, and I turned to look at who'd hit me. Sara was still in the car.

"What the hell is she doing?" B asked, his irritation with my roommate now obvious. It seemed like she was being tolerated, but barely.

"My guess is she's probably waiting for you to be a gentleman." I shrugged as I said it before giving him a look. Like he wasn't capable of acts of chivalry. "Why did you invite her?" I asked.

"I figured you lived with her." He rubbed a hand through his hair. "When she asked what we were doing, she wanted to come along." He shrugged a little at that. "I didn't want to alienate your friend and tell her no." He waved at the car, and we all saw Sara looking at us. Bryce waved a hand exaggeratedly towards the restaurant. "You coming?" he shouted.

It was hard to judge her expression, but it looked like she pulled a face as she opened the door herself. By the time she got to the three of us, she had her expression schooled into something that looked more flirtatious when she got to B's side. He would treat her like he did all the other girls who came before her.

It made me wish Sara wasn't here. I didn't want to witness him treating her like she was disposable. Just like I didn't want to witness her putting her hands all over him. But it was too late now.

We were led to a table, and I saw Noah jump up immediately. His expression looked hopeful. It'd been a few days since we had spoken. With the way I was working now, I shouldn't be surprised by the way he looked at me. There was a hint of uneasiness that he wore with his neatly pressed slacks and the crisp button down, but he offered his hand to Bryce and Lucas like he always did. They each tugged him forward in that weird one-armed hug handshake thing that men do. When he got to me, he did the same thing he always did with only a little hesitation. He kissed my cheek.

I figured the safest place for me to sit was against the wall. To save us all a headache, I didn't give anyone the opportunity to pull my chair out for me. I sat myself and looked at the rest of my party. Lucas moved to sit across from me, smirking like he knew what I was thinking. Bryce sat next to Lucas, looking ruffled. Probably because I had chosen the seat next to where Noah had already been sitting. No one gave Sara any more mind, and she looked irritated by having to sit at the end of the table.

"So, this is what you guys do?" she asked as she looked between B and Noah. "You go out to dinner with one another. This is it?"

"This is kind of what friends do," Bryce grumbled. "It's how we catch up." He waved a hand towards the group of us. "We grew up together. We didn't want to grow apart when we had to adult." He looked at me then. "We wanna stick together, so we have nights out every few weeks."

Noah nodded beside me, his face schooled to something that looked even. "Never thought you were interested in tagging along though," he directed at Sara.

"And leave Fran with all these fine men by herself? Please." She laughed in a way that irked my nerves almost immediately. She gave me a grin that I tried not to grimace at. "Sharing is caring. I just never got an invitation before."

"No kidding." Noah gave me some side-eye as he said responded to her admission. "Well, I guess that's finally changed. What do you do for a living?" He was being diplomatic, while Bryce looked bored and more than willing to ignore the girl next to him.

That's when his phone came out; it was something Bryce did when he was bored. I rolled my eyes as I expected annoying game sounds to drown out the conversation between Noah and Sara. I jumped a little when my phone vibrated in my pocket. I had it out to see a text I received from B.

'How do we get rid of the roomie?'

Lucas looked at me curiously, and I noticed he had his phone in hand, too. The text had been sent to the group. Bryce wasn't the only one who wanted her gone, it seemed.

'My best guess is to get her dinner, and then we go our separate ways?' I sent back to him.

'We were supposed to talk,' Lucas added to the conversation.

'Pick a place for us to meet up at then.' After I moment of consideration, I added, 'We could meet up at the bar for a beer?'

Bryce thumbed furiously at his phone. 'Or we could meet up at Lucas' or Noah's for a serious conversation.'

Once he was sure I read the text, he raised both eyebrows at me like he was expecting me to have an argument ready.

After the ride here and watching Sara get uncomfortably close to both Bryce and Noah, I decided 'serious conversation' probably wasn't a bad thing.

'Okay,' I replied simply.

Both of them looked at me then. The silence must have gotten the attention of Noah and Sara, because they stopped talking to look at me, too. Being friends this long, I saw Noah exchange something unspoken between the other two men. There was a nod from Bryce, and Lucas straightened up in the chair, his hand rubbing at his chin.

"What's going on?" Sara broke the moment with her question.

I didn't let it bother me, figuring it was better to not let her read too much into what was going on.

"Have you decided what you want?" I opened the menu in front of me. "This place has some great alfredo."

After opening the menu, a waitress came to our table. She was just as flirty with my guys as Sara, and I felt every little smile she gave them. I'd been worried about jealousy between the boys, and here I was glaring at everyone who dared give them a second look. I couldn't remember if I was always like this or not.

We ordered food and drinks and ate in relative silence. No one made an effort to offer conversation. This wasn't something we did often, sit in silence.

"So…" Sara noticed it and went for an ice breaker. "What do you do?"

I looked up from my noodles to see who she was talking to.

"Attorney," Noah answered around his hot wings. I didn't resist my urge to laugh at the sauce he had smeared on his face. I got a snort, and he wiped his face and fingers off with his napkin.

"Really?" She looked interested as she spoke to him. "What kind of lawyer are you?"

"Business for the most part," he answered. "I'm just a junior associate, I gotta work my way up from the bottom."

"Can't get me out of parking tickets, can you?" Sara batted her eyelashes at him as she asked.

He laughed because he had all of our attention. And while I didn't have a car, I was still curious. Bryce and Lucas, on the other hand, both drove everywhere. I knew for a fact that Bryce had a heavy foot, and Noah had never offered to help him get out of tickets.

"Sorry, I can't do that." He gave Bryce a solid look. "Even if I could do that, I wouldn't."

"Lame ass," B grumped as he went back to the burger he'd ordered.

We lingered at the table, not quite ready to call it a night. Sara seemed to be aware of it because after the plates were cleared, she got up.

"I need to hit the restroom," she said but lingered at the table, eyeing me expectantly. "You want to come with?"

I blinked, not understanding at first, then I shook my head. "I'm good. I don't have to go. Thanks."

Sara made a noise like she was put out by my refusal and left the table. As soon as she was gone, the four of us put our heads together. "You were supposed to go with her," Lucas said. "Girls are supposed to travel in packs. Safety in numbers, remember?"

"We're at a restaurant, Dad." I rolled my eyes. "Not a club. She'll perfectly fine. She's been bugging me for your numbers since not long after I moved in." I grimaced at Lucas. "I figured the main reason you were gone when I woke up the last time you crashed on the couch was because she got handsy or something."

"Definitely doesn't like keeping her hands to herself," Bryce admitted as he swiped through his phone. "She got my number earlier." He looked uncomfortable as he continued, "Chick is pretty insistent."

Noah made a face. "Does she keep putting her hand on your knee under the table, too?"

"The thirst is real." B nodded. "Either she can't seem to make up her mind who she wants, or she's hard up for all three of us." He propped his chin up in his hand and looked mildly irritated. "Why is it always the wrong chicks?"

That earned me more attention than I was prepared for. "I'm oblivious." I shrugged at them. "If you want to interrogate all my exes, they'll tell you I missed a lot of the signals they sent my way." I took a minute to eye

Lucas, then directed my attention to Bryce. "If you want something, it's usually better to be direct about it."

"Yeah, but if I'm direct with you, you're gonna think all I want is one thing." He looked pointedly at me. "If you're oblivious, I can't be subtle. But I shoot myself in the foot if I tell you what I want. How do I win, Frankie?"

It was the first time I felt like I was pinned between the three of them. They looked at me expectantly, like I had all the answers. I looked between each of them as I considered what to say and how to not be the picture they painted of Sara.

"We're here." I made sure to be just loud enough to be heard over the chatter of the restaurant. "Haven't you won already?"

"Where do we go from here then?" Lucas asked.

"You guys making plans on where to go from here?" Sara asked as she stepped up to the chair she'd been occupying before. "We gonna hit the club or something?"

"We're not the type to go out to the clubs," Lucas admitted to Sara. "We mostly just sit around a table and bullshit."

"I don't get white girl wasted," Bryce added beside her. "We don't paint each other's nails and braid our hair."

"You would look good with braids," I offered to B, unable to fight the grin.

"But you do sleepovers?" Sara asked, her attention on Noah. "Did you paint her nails when she stayed the night with you?"

That sobered the table. I put my face in my hands and considered how to put it without airing out the whole situation. Sara didn't need to know the details of it, but maybe if I admitted to sleeping with Noah, she'd stop pawing at him.

Then he laughed aloud like she'd said something funny. He gave her a grin, that dimple showing. "If you thought we slept together, why have you been getting familiar with me from the moment you sat at the table?" Despite the jovial way he spoke, the smile didn't reach his eyes. There was something about the set of his shoulders that made me straighten. Noah didn't get angry often, and I always thought he was a cool head in comparison to Bryce and me. But everything about him now overflowed anger. "Or do you normally feel up men that might be spoken for?" He raised an eyebrow at her as he asked the question, like he dared her to deny it.

"So, you're dating?" Her features only twitched a little in the face of Noah's simmering mood. "Or just sleeping together?" She shrugged and tapped her fingers along the back of the chair she'd been in. "I'm asking because it's hard to keep track of who she's with and who she's not." She tilted her head towards Bryce as she continued talking to Noah. "About a month ago, I saw him kissing her in her room. Not a week before that, blondie was crashing on our couch. You see why I'm getting confused, right? Is she with you? Or him? Or all of you?"

"She's an adult," Bryce spoke up, his expression dark. He didn't bother hiding his own anger. "Why is it your business who she's with?"

I think Sara realized then that she shot herself in the foot. No one at the table would take her side. The people she'd strong-armed into taking her out weren't willing to put up with her crap. She probably didn't consider how that would affect her getting a ride home.

Me? I was satisfied to just sit and watch her go down in flames. Lucas appeared to be in the same boat. His eyes were narrowed, and I could see him reassessing his opinion of her quietly. He leaned forward on the table and spoke lightly, "Bryce can take you home. After this, how about we just be polite in passing? No one here is going to give you that attention, so we can avoid anything embarrassing by just stopping it."

"I guess that would be the adult way to do it." Sara offered me a calculating look I could see in the dark-brown eyes that measured me. "Fran and I can talk about it later." She turned to Bryce. "Take me home."

Bryce didn't hide his distaste as he stepped away from the table.

"I'll do it." Noah got up then. "I've never gotten the chance to talk to Frankie's roommate before. I think now's a good time for me and her to get to know each other." He nodded at Lucas. "I'll give you guys a holler later."

There was a murmur of agreements, and we watched them walk out of the restaurant.

"He's taking one for the team." Bryce put a hand to his heart like it was some horrible ordeal.

"What's the plan now then?" I asked.

Bryce and Lucas exchanged a look, then stared hard at me. "The plan," Lucas began, "was to have a private conversation about what we can do and can't do."

"After Noah spilled about what you two did, it kinda left me…" Bryce paused then nodded towards Lucas. "Both of us wanting a similar opportunity."

"It doesn't necessarily have to be now. Just whenever it feels natural to you," Lucas added, taking the approach evenly where Bryce seemed eager. "Just as long as you understand what it would mean and what it wouldn't."

"What would it mean?" I asked, curious about where this would go without Noah's input.

Lucas released a breath. "It would be consummating every feeling we've had towards you."

"Giving reality to it." Bryce seemed a little less eager now when he spoke. He looked at me with the nervousness I'd seen on Noah before I had pulled him into his bedroom. "I've fantasized about you." He looked flustered now as he shared his secret. "For as long as I can remember, I never thought I'd get the chance for it to happen. But when I kissed you," he looked a little more sure of himself, "I knew the sex, hell… everything would be mind blowing with you."

"The way you suggested," Lucas started carefully. "Seems like the best route we can take without breaking up our dynamic."

That part had already been discussed, and I didn't feel like going over it all again in a public place.

"So, whose house are we going to?"

Bryce grimaced. "The walls at my apartment might as well be paper. When I get with girls who are too vocal, I get complaints."

Lucas rolled his eyes, looking like he didn't believe the other man. "We can go back to my place. You know what it looks like." He tapped the table. "Or we can all go home and call it a night. Do whatever another day."

Lucas gave me options. But if I went home now, it'd probably put me face to face with Sara in a way I didn't want to be.

"Let's go to your place." I rubbed my fingers against my temple. Even if we didn't do anything, I'd rather spend the evening talking to my friends than hiding from my roommate. "We can text Noah and figure things out like we were supposed to here."

They exchanged another look, and Bryce's excitement was obvious. Lucas looked curiously at me, but he didn't say anything as he got up. He led the way out of the restaurant. We all piled into Bryce's car when Lucas spoke up, "If we're going back to my place, it doesn't have to be all at once."

"Take turns?" Bryce asked, looking as if his complete focus was on the road. "Can I go first?"

"That's not up to you," Lucas said from the backseat. "That's up to her. Anything that happens tonight, or any other night, is up to her. We don't call those shots." Hearing it out like that was a relief. "We don't do anything she's not okay with."

The warmth I felt was something I was familiar with when it came to Lucas. It was something he induced on a number of occasions growing up. Right then, sitting in the car next to Bryce with Lucas just behind me, I realized I loved him. I loved Lucas without a doubt, and if

I'd been able to touch him, I wouldn't have been able to fight the urge.

I glanced at Bryce, and I didn't know if I had the same feeling towards him. He was my friend. There was the platonic love that I felt for him before he had ever kissed me, but I didn't know if it was more than that. There was a similar doubt with Noah. I cared about both of them, but I didn't know if the feelings I had for Lucas were the same as what I felt for them.

"I can wait," B said at last. "I mean, I've waited this long." He gave me a little smile. "As long as you know, with you... I wouldn't be one and done." He gripped the steering wheel hard enough that his knuckles turned white. "You're too important."

Warmth blossomed in me then. Regardless of the fact I was unsure about how I felt, I knew what I wanted now. "You are, too," I assured him. I glanced over a shoulder to look at Lucas. "You've had my back for so long." I sat back in the front seat and let myself get lost in the city backdrop, the cars, and buildings. Things I saw every day. "I don't know what I would do without you."

"Same." Bryce's voice was quiet, not quite a whisper. It was like he didn't want to be heard. It was comforting.

It was after eight, and I hazarded a glance over at Mom's house. The front porch light was on and so was the one that lit up the living room. It'd been a while since I last talked to her, and I should've called her when I got up this morning and given her a report as to how things were going. But I was distracted by my boys.

Nothing new there.

"Tomorrow," I promised as I followed Lucas to his front door. "I'll call her tomorrow."

"Remind me to call mine," B said as he came up beside me. "She harps at me when I go too long without getting in touch with her. I'll bet Mrs. Kemp rides Noah's ass, too."

"Do it." Lucas opened the door and waved us in. "Those missed opportunities add up when they're not there anymore."

It was a truth I didn't want to hear. Something he said with experience. As soon as we were in his house, I didn't hesitate to wrap my arms around his middle and hug him tightly. He chuckled a little, and once I looked up, I saw Bryce had the same thought.

There was a slight height difference between the two men, with Lucas being the shorter of the two. Not that it mattered much to me, I was still dwarfed by both of them. B wrapped one arm around Lucas' shoulders and the other around mine, so we were sandwiched against his chest. I relaxed against them, something I was used to. Emotional support and warmth that sometimes I didn't feel at home. And now we would push the boundaries of what we'd always had.

I looked up at Lucas with a sudden knot in my stomach, then I glanced at Bryce. If this was going to happen, I would have to initiate it. If there was ever a good opportunity to do that, it was now. I just hoped it wouldn't come off the wrong way.

I leaned against Lucas and tipped up on my toes, closing the distance to press my lips against his. I heard Bryce make a noise, and I tilted my head to one side so I could slant my mouth against Lucas' and tried to coax him to open for me. He didn't resist, but he didn't push for more. He let me kiss him without taking control.

It was heady, and I felt the brush of Bryce's breath against my ear. It must've been something for him to just watch.

"Can I kiss you, too?" Bryce asked. His voice was low in a way that it made my insides clench.

I hummed what I hoped he would take as an affirmative, and it was clear when I felt his lips against my neck. It was like he mirrored my movements but against my skin, like everything was standing on end and reacting in a rush that bled into how I kissed Lucas. I could easily feel how it affected him, pressed against him. There was no denying the growing hardness I felt against my stomach.

My hair was gathered up to one side in a fist. I couldn't tell which one of them did it, but it didn't bother me. Not when Bryce shifted, so he followed a line across the back of my neck. I broke away from Lucas' mouth when the need to breathe became too demanding. He followed Bryce's lead and was at my jaw. The bristle on his face dragging against my skin lit a fire along the path he traveled.

"Do you want it like this?" Lucas asked, pulling back just enough to speak. "Do you like being stuck between us?"

"I could do this," Bryce was quick to answer for me.

My hair fell back around my shoulders, and I felt him stoop before his hands gripped my thighs just at my knees. He hefted me up, and it felt like he wasn't even making an effort. Then he held me so that my ass was level with his hips, and I could feel just how excited he was.

He held my weight easily and had my legs parted in a way that Lucas fit easily between them. I should've been put off or at least intimidated by this. Being sandwiched between them meant that this would go one of two ways. At this height, with the way blood rushed through my ears and just how good it felt to be in this position, I was tempted to let it happen without complaint. I had never experimented with anything like this, and it wouldn't be as simple as taking just one of them in from behind. There would be discomfort, and there would be an effort I didn't know if there would be patience for.

"I could, too." Lucas pulled away from me, and I was caught up in the deep blues of his eyes. He rolled his hips against mine, rocking his hardening cock against me.

I choked on my breath, and I felt Bryce mimic the movement Lucas made. I moaned, and I could only imagine how it would feel to have them both in me at the same time. I was tempted further when they moved in sync with one another.

"We could do this to you." Bryce's mouth was at my ear, and I felt a hand cup one breast, squeezing tight enough to bring me back to focus. "Or we could do it other ways." His tongue traced along the outer shell of my ear. "Every time you talked shit to me, I'd dream about fucking that mouth. I could do that now. All the while he took you like he wants to until I got the chance to fuck that pussy, too."

"You're afraid." Lucas stilled as he watched me with narrowed eyes. "What are you afraid of?"

"I don't know that I could handle it," I admitted. While Lucas was okay with stopping to discuss this with me, Bryce was distracted with my ear. And my boob, too, as it seemed he was the one pawing it.

"Then tell us to stop." Lucas didn't even flinch, he thumped Bryce's forehead. "That's all you have to do."

The hand on my breast tightened briefly before he released it altogether. I heard the wince behind me, then felt the way his chest seemed to deflate. I tilted my head back so I could rest it on his shoulder and decided to clarify before I was treated to the kick puppy look.

"I don't know that I could handle you both at once. This now, the touching and kissing, is nearly overwhelming. Sex with both of you? At the same time?" I released a breath and tangled a hand in Lucas' hair. "I doubt I could handle it." My hand dropped from his hair, down to cup the side of his face. The hair there wasn't necessarily sandpaper quality, but it was coarse. It tickled my palm, and I already knew how it felt to be brushed against my chin and cheek. How would it feel to brush against other places? "But I don't want you to stop."

Lucas' lips twitched. He had a hand on my hip, and it squeezed me to the point of being near painful. "Then let's go to one of the few rooms I have finished in this damn house." With that said, Lucas let me go and left me being held against Bryce.

"Are you sure?" Bryce whispered in my ear. "Please, please don't change your mind about this." There was a hint of desperation in his voice, and I could feel it in the hum of his body behind mine.

"I'm sure," I said gently, wiggling from his grasp. He made a noise of protest, but when I turned to him, he welcomed me, hefting me up high enough so I could kiss away his worries. He didn't seem to have any issues with just kissing me in the front room of Lucas' house.

"Don't fuck her against the sheetrock, asshole," Lucas called from down the hall. "The first time you have with Frankie is going to be in a fucking bed. After that, you can fuck her against all the walls in my house."

Bryce pulled away from me and hollered back to our friend at the end of the hallway, "I'm going to hold you to that." He put me down and bent to give me a light kiss. "But first, a bed." He turned then to lead the way to Lucas' bedroom.

I lingered in the sheetrocked-but-otherwise-bare living room, looking at Lucas where he stood in the hallway.

"Only if you want it, Frankie," he said without the same air of fear that Bryce had. While Lucas may want me just as much as Bryce did, he had patience. He would wait until he thought I was ready. He would wait his turn.

Lucas was so good to all of us.

"I want this," I assured him as I made my way over the subflooring. I pulled up the hem of the sequined shirt I'd been wearing. By the time I got to Lucas, I had it over my head. When I had the silky cloth off, I met his gaze again. He hadn't glanced down to see the bra I wore or my breasts. He looked at me. "I want you," I said with honesty that I felt in my stomach. Or maybe the throbbing knot above it. I looked into the bedroom where Bryce stood watching the two of us. "I want him, too."

Bryce didn't have any qualms looking at my breasts. He never did. Fortunately, at the sight of me without a shirt, he tugged his up and off without any attempt at being sexy. He started on his belt and had his jeans open before he thought better of it. He looked at me and rubbed his hand at his neck, giving me an eyeful of defined muscles that made my mouth go dry. Now I saw why he went through women so easily—B had a nice body.

"How do we do this?" he asked, knocking me out of my reverie.

"I can watch," Lucas offered behind me. He stepped closer to me. "Unless you have other ideas?"

"Watch?" I parroted back to him, and I heard Bryce echo me, "What do you mean watch?"

"You're not gonna participate?" Bryce asked hurriedly after me. His hands wandered, going from rubbing at his neck to resting on his hips. They were nervous ticks I hadn't seen on him in so long. "I thought we were all gonna be involved." He paused, and I glanced at him to see him fidget more. "I'm not much for performing for an audience."

Lucas laughed a little at that before tugging his shirt up. "Just go ahead like you were before. I'll fit in where I can without making her uncomfortable. But I ain't worried about your ass."

I got just as distracted by Lucas as I was with Bryce. He had worked to build and maintain his body for sports with equipment that had been supplied by schools. While it was hard work, it was hard work that came from a gym. Lucas might not have the full definition and clean lines that Bryce did, but I knew his lean lines came from a lifetime of hard work. Nothing was ever easy for him, and here he was taking a side step so Bryce could go first.

I took Lucas' hand. "You can touch me and kiss me while he and I are…" I stalled out there, suddenly unable to call it what it was. I didn't have a good excuse for why I was floundering right there. Nerves, maybe? I didn't want to call it fucking; it sounded so crass, and I didn't want that feeling.

"We'll have fun," Lucas assured me and pushed me closer in Bryce's direction.

Bryce hesitated at first, but I could see it when he decided to throw everything to the wind. He cupped my face and tugged me forward into a hungry kiss. It was like he threw fire on top of that first kiss he'd given me in my bedroom. His lips drew me in and burned everything in me. Then I felt two hands come up behind me to cup my breasts, and a mouth fell on my shoulder. God, I wanted it. I wanted them.

And I could have all three of them without consequence.

My bra came loose, and one of them shoved it down and out of the way. The different textures of skin brushing against mine lost me. I touched as I was touched. I traced lines until I felt the rough material of jeans, and I delved into them. Bryce's mouth broke away from mine when my hand closed around his erection.

"Careful." His breath hitched a little bit. "I might have hyped myself up for this a little too much. That's got a hair trigger on it."

I felt Lucas' laugh quake against my back, and then a set of hands reached down to open my jeans, distracting me. "I figured when she got angry with you, it would've calmed your ass down," he said as he brushed the rough hair on his face against my neck.

"Never been able to control it when she gets pissed at me," Bryce admitted, and I decided to test the theory by giving him a squeeze. I watched as his features crumpled, and I got an answering throb from the cock in my hand. "Goddamn," he hissed out.

"So much for foreplay," Lucas snickered. "How are you going to get her hot and bothered enough to take that?" As he asked, he slipped his hand into my jeans. The heat of his hand cutting through my pubic hair put me on the same edge I knew Bryce danced on. My breath caught as I felt him fully cup me, and I knew I wouldn't be able to give the man in front of me any grief.

"That's what you're here for, boss." Bryce's voice was husky. "Knees, man," he gritted out. "If I'm gonna make any good effort at throwing it, I'm gonna need to speed this along now."

"Get on the bed," Lucas instructed, and before I could follow it, he had my jeans and panties down around my ankles. I kicked off my tennis shoes and moved to help Bryce shuck the rest of his clothes.

Bryce pulled me along as we went towards the head of the bed before he collapsed back, tugging me on top of him. I didn't wait for any further prompting, I straddled his hips and bent down to kiss him with the same kind of fervor he'd shown from the beginning. His cock was pressed against me, hard and throbbing against my heat in just the right way that I wouldn't have any qualms about adjusting so he could slide right in.

"Rubbers, dumbasses," Lucas broke through my lust-filled haze. And if the grip on my hips were any sort of hint, Bryce was just as irritated by it as I was. "Wrap it up." He tossed a handful of foil packs onto the bed. "I can only imagine how Frankie's mom would be if she found out she was knocked up and couldn't figure out who the dad was. Can you imagine how yours would be if she found out you knocked up Frankie?"

"Mama would murder me," I admitted, sobering up enough to search for one of the condoms in the tangled bedspread. "She'd beat my ass like she's never beat it before. Not to mention she wouldn't be happy about any of this." I found one of the little foil squares and ripped it open without a second thought. "She always thought you three were a bad influence on me."

I shifted backward onto Bryce's thighs, rolling the latex onto his cock with a clinical edge that only residency would induce. I was getting ready to spear myself on him, to fill that void in me that craved this like a junkie. Arms came around me as I adjusted Bryce's cock to take aim at my entrance.

"Not so fast," Lucas' purred low in my ear, keeping me from settling down on the man below me. He was pressed behind me, and I could feel his own erection pressed into the curve of my ass. "Take your time, Frankie. This is something we're supposed to savor, not rush into." He had his free hand between my thighs before I could protest, and I felt a finger dip into me. "Not nearly wet enough to go diving right on him like that. I want this to be memorable, not painful."

Bryce sat up, and I felt surrounded by them. "I've waited this long," he breathed before turning his attention to my breasts. "I can wait long enough for this to be good for you, too." He pressed my breasts up and together, then laved his tongue over each in turn before he settled for latching onto a nipple. I felt the pull of his mouth where Lucas' fingers teased me.

Since Bryce had both of my breasts occupied, Lucas moved his other hand between my thighs. Fingers pressed into me while another circled the bundle of nerves at the same time. Coupled with Bryce's teasing mouth, I couldn't restrain any noise I made. My hips rolled with abandon, and I keened with every overwhelming touch.

I'd never been one to sleep around, the hard eye of my mother and my first misadventure with sex had always been a deciding factor. But now, with the sure work of Lucas' fingers and Bryce's wandering mouth, I found myself realizing just what I'd been missing out on. Being with Noah had been good, especially considering how good he'd been with his mouth and hands. But this was a level of experience I'd never been on before. Nothing kept me from tumbling apart from the combined affections.

When I melted between them, Lucas deftly removed his fingers from me and rumbled into my ear about how beautiful I was. With a little maneuvering from Bryce, I felt the head of his cock at my entrance. I was still flying high from the orgasm both gave me, so I didn't object that I needed a moment to recover.

I wrapped my arms around the man in front of me and clenched as he stretched me. He filled me to the point of it being dizzying, it felt so good. I ached, and the throb from before was back, only to get an echo of it from the cock within me. His groan quaked through me, and he curled further against my chest as Lucas and I shifted me further down onto him.

"Wait, wait," Bryce gritted out. His hands on my hips tightened to the point of near pain. "Wait!" It was a desperate plea. "Goddamn. I'm not fuckin' sixteen. I won't bust." He wasn't talking to either of us; it was clear he directed it at himself. If I'd been anyone else, I would've probably been judgmental, but I had an idea of where he was at. This was something he'd wanted so much, his control wasn't where it usually was.

"Don't strive for a marathon," Lucas said from behind me. He'd kept his hand between Bryce and me, and when his fingers circled me again, I didn't stifle anything. "You got me waiting for you to finish. Plus, if you're gonna be a quick shot, I'm gonna make sure she gets a happy ending."

"I'm not a fuckin' quick shot." Bryce's head shot up as he snapped it. His hands left my hips, and he cupped my face. "Fuckin' look at me, Frank." My eyes opened, and I saw something in his brown eyes that I didn't expect. It took me back to when I was with Noah. "This ain't gonna be enough for me." It came out of him as a promise. "I need you."

I felt a knot in my throat, and I didn't know how to respond to that. I'd never had the afterthought of going without any of my boys, but if this admission was Bryce's feelings for me, he would want something in return.

"You got me," I tried to assure him, but my voice sounded choked. That knot.

A hand went back down to my hip, and Bryce's hips rolled up into mine. I bounced a little, but there wasn't much space to move. Not with the way I was being held by both men, the way I was surrounded. But with the movement within me, and the ever-persistent circling of my clit, it had me drowning in the feelings they'd invoked before Bryce penetrated me. Now it was magnified.

B tilted back for leverage, and the hand on my face dropped. His expression closed, and his hips worked up a short, choppy rhythm that still managed to work me into a steady burn. With the building burn, Bryce put more force behind his hips. Before long, his breath hitching and pained noises came from him.

"Fuck," hissed between his teeth, and I didn't try to look away. I resisted closing my eyes so I could watch as he fell apart. I got lost in it, watching him. He flopped backward on the bed, throwing his hips upward in a stuttered rhythm before he stiffened.

I was caught off guard when I was forced off the edge with him. I didn't get the chance to come down this time either, as Lucas' fingers went from circling my clit to strumming it as if it were a string on a guitar. He pushed me along it until I was whining for a break.

"Oh fuck," Bryce croaked under me. "So hot."

"Please," I whimpered. I was over-sensitized, and every swipe of his fingers made me twitch. Lucas pulled his hands away, caressing my thighs and kissing the side of my face. It was probably the best way I could come down. "I think you're ruining sex for me."

"In a bad way?" Lucas asked. "Between the three of us, I'm the one with blue balls."

"Give me a minute." I reached back to pinch his thigh. "I can't feel my toes, and I don't think my legs are going to hold me."

"I am perfectly happy to stay ball deep in her," Bryce commented from the lazy puddle of man he'd turned into. "Don't think I'm gonna be able to move. I don't want to."

"Bed isn't big enough for you to loaf," Lucas said as he wrapped his arms around my middle, up under my arms, and he carefully eased me off of Bryce. "Besides, I had your back, making sure she got off. You could do me the same."

"Yeah, yeah," Bryce groaned as he pulled out of me. "Just let me catch my breath."

"That's fine," Lucas breathed and turned me so he could lie down on my back. He settled against my side, turning me so he could kiss me. I melted into his side, splaying a hand against his chest and drowning in the feel of his mouth on mine. The feelings that welled up in me for the man who I was against were just as overwhelming as when I was surrounded by Lucas and Bryce.

He touched me as he kissed me, and one arm was curled around me, holding me close. His hand drifted down my side, swirling at my hip before coming to cup my ass. It was like every cell was alive for him, and I was drunk on that feeling alone.

The bed shifted, and I found myself eager to have Bryce's hands on me, too. I could drown in this overwhelming feeling of multiple hands on me, of more than one mouth finding ways to light me on fire. This was definitely something that would skew my view of sex.

"Your phone is ringing." Bryce broke through the haze of emotion and feelings that Lucas induced. "I bet it's Noah."

"I didn't even hear it," Lucas said as he pulled away from me. His nose brushed against mine. "Gimme a minute." He pulled away from me, and it was like a static reaction with the separation, little pops of electricity I felt along my side and every bit of skin he touched.

I sat up, trying not to let the loss bother me, and watched as he fished through the pile of clothes to find his phone. I took the chance to appreciate the naked view it offered me of Lucas. He was crouched down, and I caught sight of the erection I'd only ever felt. His cock hung heavily towards the floor. He was larger than I would've guessed, and I swallowed hard. My mind swirled with all the silly questions and thoughts of whether I'd be able to take all of him into me or not. If it would hurt. I knew better, I was wet enough after being between the two of them that there should be little issue.

"Fuck." Lucas stood with his phone in hand and thumbed over the screen. With a little bit of finessing, he had it ringing so all three of us could hear.

"It's about damn time," Noah answered. "I have been calling for the last ten minutes."

"We were busy," Bryce answered.

There was a minute of silence, then a sigh. "You assholes couldn't wait for me to get there?"

"You did volunteer to take Sara home." I flopped back on the bed as I said it. I might as well take advantage of this intermission while I could. "You should've let B take her home if you wanted in on the fun."

"Hey," Bryce squawked beside me, poking my side. "That was fucking good. Don't you act like that wasn't good."

"Damnit!" Noah's voice echoed through the room.

"It's only right," Lucas interjected. "You've already had your turn. You got to let the rest of us get ours." He looked at me and came to the bed. I watched, suddenly distracted as he crawled onto it. The look he gave me had everything standing at attention. He prowled until he was over me. "You can be the caboose if you get here before she passes out. Are you gonna object to having a train run on you?"

"If it's worth my while, can I complain?" It was the only thing I could think to say. It was bravado I shouldn't have, considering how I hadn't been in this position before.

"Is she drunk?" I heard Noah ask. "I can't believe she'd be willing for all three of us in one night."

"I didn't drink," I assured him. "But I've got Lucas over me. I can't promise he won't wear me out before you get here."

"I'll be ten minutes," Noah barked before ending the call.

I looked up at Lucas then. He was still hovered over me, and I felt the throb of need in me return. His eyes were hooded, and I could see just how much he wanted me without having to glance down at his erection.

"Why did we wait so long to do this?" I asked. I couldn't fathom a reason right now.

"Priorities." He released a breath. "I might've had mine wrong. We'll have to see."

He lowered himself down on me and kissed me again. There was a little less heat behind it but no less emotion. I wrapped my arms around his shoulders and dug my fingers into his hair.

"Fuck priorities," I managed when he gave me a chance to get a breath. I felt the bed quake when Bryce laughed.

"Only priorities we should all have," Bryce snickered, "is remembering to keep it wrapped up." He produced one of the little foil squares that had been flung onto the bed before.

I was quick to pluck it up and ripped open the wrapper. I was way too eager for this. B's reminder didn't cause any sort of disruption; it just added fuel to my fire. I found that Lucas' erection was pressed between us, and I felt the beat of his heart through it. It was a little effort to roll the latex onto him, and he didn't seem bothered by me touching him in the way Bryce had. I gave him a measured stroke, watching his face for any tells that he might be sitting on a similar edge.

Lucas raised his chin a little but made no move to stop me. There was a rumbling in his chest as I gave him a light squeeze with my fist. I was tempted to keep stroking, but I didn't want to shift the condom. I shouldn't have been so quick to roll the latex on.

"Next time…" he breathed lightly, like he could see what I wanted to do. "Next time we won't be in any kind of a rush."

"Next time," Bryce started, and I turned to see him watching. He was on his side facing us, his head propped up on a hand. "There'll be more time to touch and taste everything. Noah said he went down on you." He closed his eyes, then seemed to pointedly lick his lips. "Said it was the best pussy he'd ever eaten."

My breath caught, and I tried not to let it distract me too much. "We don't need foreplay," I said to Lucas. "I'm too impatient," I admitted. "I want you in me."

The only indication Lucas felt anything from my words was the twitch of his eyebrows. His cock throbbed, so I knew I had its attention at least.

"I don't want to rush fucking you," he said lightly.

"Noah will be here soon," Bryce supplied. "Only time to get a solo entrance." It was like he was encouraging Lucas to hurry.

"Take me," I breathed, and I could see his eyes dilate. "Lucas," I moaned a little for emphasis.

For all my show of need, he seemed to have no issues with taking his time. He wedged his knee between my thighs and settled slowly against me. I rolled my hips up against him, trying to encourage him to get into the right position, so he could slide into me. The movement affected him more than anything else, and his eyes fluttered closed as he rolled his hips against mine. I clenched, feeling the heat and the emptiness.

"I need you," I keened.

"Are you insatiable?" Bryce asked. It wasn't entirely distracting, but it seemed out of nowhere. "Is that why you can handle both of us?"

"I wanted both of you," I managed through the lust. "I want all three of you," I whimpered. "Please, Lucas."

With a little maneuvering of his hips, I felt the push of his cock against my entrance. I arched up, trying to push him into me.

"Say please again." Lucas' eyes narrowed at me. "You want me," his voice was a low growl. "Say it again."

"Please," it came out of me with a breath.

He thrust into me then, a quick one instead of the slow entrance Bryce had given me earlier. I choked on the breath I'd been taking, and I didn't get the chance to make an appropriate noise. I didn't get the chance to adjust, either. Lucas kept moving. He built a steady rhythm that was hard and fast, and it left me struggling for a handle to hold onto and to remember to keep breathing.

He pushed himself up on his arms, and the angle changed. Somehow he managed to get deeper even though he already had me so full. Every movement he made brought a cry out of me, but then a hand came in and teased the bundle of nerves at the top of my sex. A hand was also on my breast, and that overwhelming feeling of when I'd been between both men returned. Now I was just beneath Lucas, but Bryce followed his lead and teased me while the other man penetrated me.

The bedroom door opened and, at first, no one reacted. Lucas kept moving, and Bryce kept touching me in a way that had my toes curling. I flexed my thighs around Lucas' hips and danced on an edge I don't think I'd been on before.

"I fucking said ten minutes." Noah's complaint brought it all to a screeching halt. He stood in the doorway watching with an air of jealousy like he hadn't been in a position like this with me before.

"You knew what we were doing when you called," Bryce said lazily, bending down to latch onto the breast closest to him. He didn't seem bothered at all by the interruption. Maybe because he'd been able to enjoy himself before Noah even called.

"You locked the front door, right?" Lucas asked, his hips stilling as he looked at the other man. "We don't need anyone else coming into this."

"I did," Noah snapped as he tugged his shirt up and over his head, not bothering with the buttons. He came to the side of the bed to look at me—us—and sighed. "I get to join in, right?" He directed the question at me.

I didn't have words to answer him, so I reached out to grab the front of his slacks. I remembered the feel of his mouth on me. Noah let me open his belt and pants, and I reached in to pull his hardening cock out. Just as I closed my lips around the head of him, Lucas moved again. I moaned, and I heard Noah echo me. It was heady.

I tried to stay afloat long enough to take more of Noah's cock into my mouth. His hips bucked forward, and I nearly choked on him. Breathing took effort with everything going on. Fingers moved on my clit again, while Lucas moved with the same ferocity he had started with. I couldn't fight the feelings bubbling up in me.

I couldn't keep up with trying to give Noah head either, so when his hand knotted in my hair, and his hips took control, I didn't fight that either. I relaxed and let him shove his cock deeper down my throat and just fought to keep breathing. Then fingers pinched my clit, and everything broke apart. Lucas barked out an expletive and went rigid over me, quaking as he came.

"My turn?" It sounded like Noah asked, but I was still in a daze. He pulled out of my mouth, and I moaned as Lucas pulled out of me. "Finally," he growled before I was flipped. I was still putty and had no way of complaining at the shift in position. When Noah thrust into me from behind, any complaints I had in mind were immediately gone.

I rode it out, spasming as Noah rocked into me from behind. Every nerve ending was raw and rolling to another near-blinding experience. I couldn't continue this, going from one man right to another. If Bryce intended for another go, he'd find nothing but a puddle of me to work with.

I hugged the bedspread to me and held on, trying to keep myself together so Noah didn't fuck me into oblivion. He was close, I could feel it in the way he stuttered and how tight his hands were on my hips. Giving him head beforehand was likely a saving grace. It would be something I would have to remember for the next time we did this.

Because there would be a next time. There would have to be. I was probably ruined for having sex with just one man ever again.

Noah groaned behind me, long and loud. "That's twice now," Bryce said from beside me. "I feel like this isn't fair that you got to get in on this."

"Shh," I managed. Noah unsteadily pulled out of me, and I felt him flop onto the bed. I didn't see where he landed. I was stuck where I was at, nerves still humming with that high that my boys had induced. It left my ass in the air, but I couldn't find the ability to care. "No fighting."

Someone pushed me onto my side, and I felt an arm wrap around my middle. "He's had you in his bed, and now so has Lucas," Bryce whispered against my ear. "I want you in my bed, too."

"We got time," Lucas said, and I felt a hand travel over the length of my side. "Don't we, Frankie?"

"As long as you let me sleep," I groaned, perfectly fine with lying against Bryce.

"We're talking about this," Lucas said. "We got to figure out a way to do this where we're all happy, and it's not a matter of fighting over who gets Frankie and who doesn't." He gave my hip a light smack, the sting of his hand sending a tremor through my already frayed nerves.

I didn't want to think about where that could go. He slapping my ass and how I'd react. It definitely had caught something's attention. I cracked an eye open to see him lounging beside me, though he sat up against the wall.

"Let me sleep," I growled. "You guys don't get to fuck me like that and not let me recoup afterward."

"Fine." Lucas made a noise as he said it, a clear show that he was being impatient. "Tomorrow then we'll talk about it."

"Sleepover!" I felt Bryce grin

My grunt was less enthused than it should've been, considering this was the first time I'd been with the three of them. I should be analyzing it and considering where we would go from here. But all I felt was mush. Like they'd literally fucked my brains out.

Mornings were for analyzing and overthinking. Nights were for basking in the aching muscles and warm feeling that only having an arm wrapped around you could do.

10

I woke up to the sound of a shower running. I grunted and rolled over into Bryce who snorted loudly and shifted to accommodate me. He was warm, and he smelled of sweat and sex. A musk hung in the air around us. It wasn't a bad smell, and it wasn't something that repulsed me. I often heard about how the smell of sex was supposed to be disgusting or full of disappointment. None of that was here.

I reached a hand out, and it connected with a hip. The owner rolled over, and an arm went around me. I didn't have to look to know it was Noah. I smelled him just as I had Bryce. It was just as comforting.

I could've gone right back to sleep, at peace with the position I was in. I should have been able to. But my bladder chose that moment to get my attention. I tried to ignore it; I clenched my thighs together and tried to assure my bladder that it could wait.

It protested louder.

I couldn't ignore it, or stifle the need to pee, so I got up. Neither of the men still in the bed seemed to notice. I went to the bathroom, not giving the shower a second look. I found the toilet in a tiny closet, looked to make sure the seat was down, and gave in to my bladder's persistent demands. I sighed as the aches from last night caught up with me.

My hips and pelvis hurt, and my lady bits were tender in a way I'd never felt before. There was something to this mild discomfort… something that brought on an odd sense of satisfaction.

I flushed the toilet, and I heard a curse. *Oops.* I came out of the little closet to see Lucas glaring at me through the glass of the shower. I should've felt bad, but I only grinned at him. I gave myself a look in the mirror above the sink and seeing my knotted-up sex hair, I decided to step into the shower with him uninvited.

"This a round two?" he asked as he moved aside so I could get under the hot spray of water. "Because I wouldn't say no to that." He smiled a little bit, and when I turned around, I felt him work his fingers into my tangled hair.

"I think I might need a few days to recover," I admitted before turning back to him. "You guys wore me out."

"That a complaint?" He shifted me out of the water so he could rinse himself again.

"That's being realistic," I said to him, taking the opportunity to 'help' him rinse. Nothing like an opportunity to touch him in a way I hadn't been able to before.

He stilled. "Are you hurt?"

"Sore," I corrected. "A few days, and I'll be fine."

Lucas hummed lightly, then put his hands on my shoulders. He turned me to face the tiled wall. His hands drifted down my arms, then he tugged them up, and I put my hands on the wall. "Keep them there," he instructed before leaving me. I glanced over a shoulder to see him pouring soap into a palm. He came back to me and rubbed it into my shoulders. His thumbs followed the line of my spine from my neck down.

I groaned as he took his time washing my back. He found every knot and ache, things that weren't from last night. He would make me into a puddle again, but I wouldn't object.

He didn't stop at my back, though the massage ended there. His hands came around to cup my breasts, spreading soap on them and teasing them to the point I reconsidered my claim about needing a few days. He didn't tease the nipples as they tightened, but his hands drifted down, and I took a breath, hoping he would find his way between my thighs.

I wanted him. So much at that point.

He didn't give in to me. Not even when I pressed back against him and felt the twitch of his cock against my ass. I had his attention. But he wasn't giving me anything.

His hands went down my thighs and back up again. His thumbs brushed against my pubic hair, lighting everything on fire. I decided I wasn't waiting for him to give in, to give me what I wanted.

I pushed off the wall and turned to him, catching his mouth with mine and putting every ounce of hunger I felt in that moment into it. I wanted him, and I would have him despite what I said earlier. Lucas didn't pull away or fight it. He let me kiss him, and I felt every inch of his reaction swell against me.

Then he pulled away. "You said you needed a few days." His voice was hoarse. "You'll have to wait."

"I don't want to." I moved to kiss him again, but a hand in my hair pulled me to a stop.

"No." His voice went hard then. "You'll wait. You'll recoup, and then when there's another opportunity, I'll fuck your brains out."

"Fuck them out now," I demanded.

"No." He laughed a little. "I've wanted you for as long as I can remember." He drew closer, and I thought he might kiss me again. I hoped he might. But it was just a tease of his lips brushing against mine. "I've waited this long, now you can wait."

"You never said anything," I said, feeling angry with the fact he keyed me up and now denied me. "You never gave me any sign that you wanted to be anything more than my friend. If I didn't know how you felt, what I was supposed to do about it?"

"Nothing," he said gently and stepped away from me. "Wash your hair." He stepped out of the shower and pulled a towel from a cabinet. He took his time drying his hair and himself before he spoke again, "Finish up, and we'll have that talk I wanted last night." There was command in his voice as he wrapped the towel around his waist.

Lucas left me in the bathroom. Irritated, I took my time to wash my hair, using a healthy glob of his shampoo. I did my best to get the knots out with my fingers before I rinsed. Once finished, I found a fluffy white towel readily available. Lucas stuck with neutral colors like most men. The only pop of color in the bathroom was a mosaic of blue tiles that cut through the already cream and wood tones.

Once I wrapped the borrowed towel around me, I stepped into the bedroom to face whatever talk Lucas had in mind. Bryce was still stretched out on the bed, though it was clear he was awake—he wasn't snoring anymore. But apparently, he wasn't in any hurry to get moving.

Noah was already up and getting dressed in the same clothes he wore the night before. He had his slacks on and was seated on the bed, pulling on socks like he was getting ready to go.

Lucas already had a pair of shorts on, and he didn't wait for me to get dressed, though he threw the shirt he had in his hands at me. I tugged it over my head and dropped the towel. The shirt went to my thighs, so it didn't seem like a big deal. But there was something about it that got Bryce and Noah's attention.

"You wanted to talk?" I prompted.

"Where do we go from here?" Lucas started and took his time, looking at each of us. "It's not practical for us to do last night on the regular."

"I'm not opposed to doing it monthly," I cut in. "I wouldn't write that off completely. Maybe with some time figuring out the mechanics, we could have the four of us together, so it's not just a train to the point where I pass out." I paused to reconsider my words, and I raised a hand. "Not that last night wasn't good, it was. I just… I'm not a porn star. I'm gonna get worn out pretty quick bouncing between the three of you."

"You said you were sore," Lucas objected.

"I am," I snapped at him. "But that doesn't mean I didn't enjoy myself."

"Once a month sounds good to me," Bryce added, having sat up and watched the exchange with more than a little bit of interest. He had bed head that suited him, and

I tried not to get distracted by it. I wanted to stay on point for whatever arguments Lucas had. "I mean we have our bi-weekly meetups, why not just tap one of those for a gang bang?"

That threw me off, and I felt embarrassment flooding my cheeks. "That wasn't a gang bang."

"It was pretty close," Bryce said as he shrugged.

"Stop," I snapped at him. "It wasn't." I don't know why it made me angry, but here I was worried about the label. It made it sound vulgar, and I didn't think it was. I didn't want it to be.

Lucas put a hand on my shoulder like he could take the edge off my anger. "That bothers you?" His voice was low, near a whisper. He looked at me for a beat then back to Bryce. "Maybe this isn't a good idea."

"Wait, you expect shit to go back to normal after that?" Bryce waved back to the bed as if it would make the memory of last night fresh. "I can't do that." He looked at me desperate. "I can't do that. Can you even do that? Are you gonna be able to walk away after finally kissing her? Fucking her? I can't go backward."

"I don't think I can either," Noah said gently. He looked at me and stepped closer. Concern was evident in the way he stood, and he looked as if he were approaching a spooked animal. "You said there was no going backward," he directed at me then looked at Lucas. "Can you?"

I looked at Lucas, too. I didn't have an answer for the two of them. But what about Lucas?

"I will do," he looked at me, "what's necessary for us. If it means forgetting last night, then I will. I will do what's necessary for our friendship to continue."

"I love you." The words came out of me in a breath, barely audible to my own ears. "I have forever." I looked away from Lucas to Bryce; his eyes were huge, and there was something askance on his face. I knew then it wasn't directed just at the man beside me. I looked to Noah and saw something similar on his face, too. "All three of you," I clarified and knew it to be true. "I can't go backward."

"Good," Lucas murmured, his voice hoarse. "But what now?"

"Continue as we have been," Noah offered lightly. "The only things that would be different is that sex will be included in our dynamic." He stepped closer, and I couldn't tell if he was directing his words at me or at Lucas, but I paid attention anyway. "Your feelings for her aren't changed, even after seeing her with me or Bryce. Right?"

"Yeah." I looked to Lucas as he spoke. "But I'm more concerned about the outcome later. How are you going to handle all three of us on top of your career?" He shook his head. "Relationships with just one person are hard enough. But three? What was the last relationship you had that worked?" He directed the question at each of us, and there was a pointed look I couldn't meet.

"We've maintained healthy relationships with each other," I spoke up when no one else seemed willing to. I kept my eyes on the floor as I did. "We've supported each other on so many occasions throughout the years that I know damn well, as long as I have the three of you at my back, I can do anything." I took a breath as I tried to remember the textbook definition of what we were. I hadn't read a psychology book in months. "I share everything with you. If something monumental happens, then one of you, or all three of you, are the first people I need to confide in about it. I don't think I've ever been able to keep a secret from any of you." I waved a hand helplessly. "The only thing that kept us from being romantic was sex… and now we've crossed that line." I put my full attention on Lucas then. "The only difference between you guys and every other failed relationship I've been in is that I want to be with you. Any other man has always lacked something to the point where I never had even a reason to be sad about their leaving."

"Same," Bryce said simply. It was something he'd admitted to me before. No one measured up to me in his eyes. Now I saw what he was talking about.

"So now we end our phone calls with 'I love you,' and part ways with kisses?" Lucas asked, and I found that I couldn't read his expression.

"If that's what you want?" I offered back. I phrased it like a question because I couldn't tell what he was thinking.

"Maybe I do," he shot back. "Maybe Bryce does or maybe Noah does. What happens when we do? How are you going to react?"

"I just told you I love you," I snapped. "Do you think I don't mean it?"

"Platonically, yeah. You mean it." He stepped closer, and it was clear that the argument was between him and me. Bryce and Noah were just spectators now. "But what if I tell you I love you, and I don't mean it as just a friend that I'm gonna occasionally have sex with?"

"Great." My voice rose as I spoke. "I don't either. When I say I love you, I meant it like that. I love you," I shouted at him. "I loved you before we fucked, and I love you after."

"But do you love me, too?" Noah asked, putting himself back in the conversation.

"Obviously," I said in the same tone, my voice bouncing off the bare bedroom walls and back at me. And before Bryce could speak, I turned to glare at him. "That includes you, too." He just grinned at me.

"So it's decided," Bryce said as he got up. "Do we sing kumbaya? Are we gonna braid each other's hair? Because I think that just settles everything." He went through the clothes on the floor before he found his own. "How about we keep things simple? We do like we usually do and if sex happens, yay!" He had his boxers up around his hips when he looked back at Lucas. "We don't need to over-complicate things. It's never been complicated before, why make it that way now?"

"It shouldn't be that easy," Lucas argued. "Sex is supposed to complicate things. Feelings, these feelings, aren't supposed to be that easy."

"Why shouldn't it be when it works?" I asked, letting go of the irritation I felt before. "Why deviate from what works? Why can't we just add to it?"

He looked unsure before he relaxed visibly. "This is already decided," he said lightly. "No going backward then… let's just do our best to not make this a horrible decision."

"The only horrible decision we've made is waiting to take this on," Bryce said as he went back to getting dressed. "We should've done this sooner. Because I don't know about you guys, but this seems like it was the natural way to go."

Bryce was flippant about it. He had an easy acceptance that everything would just fall into place. But it felt like he was right. Like this would be easier than any other relationship I'd ever been in.

11

I walked in the door with an ache still between my thighs. Despite the long drive from Lucas' house to my apartment, I still ached. It didn't lose that satisfying edge, but I felt like I'd need a hot soak in the tub. I'd never had anything like last night before, and I knew there'd be plenty of opportunities for me to adjust to it.

That was something for another day. I needed a few days before I could even consider hitting up one of my boys. I tossed my keys into the bowl on the little table by the door and went for the bathroom. All I could think about was that hot water soak.

"Have another slumber party?" Sara stood in the kitchen by the sink, and something about the expression on her face I didn't like.

I paused, and it left me in the middle of the living room. I could ignore her and just go on into the bathroom like I wanted. If I did that, she'd draw her own conclusions. But then she might've already guessed what went on. What did it matter that she knew? If she did, would that mean she'd stop flirting with them?

"Yeah," I said and turned towards her. "We had a big ole slumber party." I waited for her to pass judgment, for her to give me some sort of smartass remark about how I was a greedy bitch, and I needed to learn how to share my toys.

Her brows went up, and she leaned back against the sink, making me think she hadn't expected me to admit it. Even though I didn't say what was done, I could tell by the way she eyed me that she went there. Sara shrugged a shoulder and went back to putting her lunch together. I took that as a dismissal.

It surprised me, but I went into the bathroom to start the tub anyhow. I let the water run and went to get a change of clothes. When I saw Sara still in the kitchen with her phone in hand, something in my stomach dropped. It wasn't so much her judgment that I was worried about, it was the attention this would bring to me.

We didn't have the same circles of friends, so I wasn't worried about that. But... what if this got back to the hospital? Was there a chance this could kill any of my aspirations? Would it affect my residency?

They couldn't fire me, I knew that. My outside life couldn't and shouldn't affect my education. But if this was something she was airing out on the internet, there was a big chance it could come back to bite me in the ass.

I took a bundle of clothes into the bathroom with my phone. I sat on the toilet seat and struggled with who I could confide my worries to. Who I could tell all my fears without having to put a strain on what we'd discussed before. Frustrated, I typed up in our group text that Sara knew. I figured it was better to just tell it to all three of them and face the consequences now rather than it get passed down the line to face later.

I set my phone down and undressed, ignoring it as it chimed on the sink with each response. I didn't look at it until I sank down into the hot water. One glance was enough to calm my nerves.

'Fuck her.' B had been the first to respond. 'Bitch is just jealous.'

'Everything'll be all right. If she tries to give you issues about it, I'll make sure she gets real close and uncomfortable with the consequences of slander.' Noah was quick to follow up with another tidbit, 'What she might know doesn't put you in any kind of awkward position. Aside from having to live with her.'

'We'll face it together.' Lucas' response was the last to round out the group of messages.

I set the phone down on the floor, feeling better. I relaxed back to enjoy my bath. This was just proof that the decision to take our friendship to something more was the right one. Sara knowing that I was sleeping with my boys wouldn't change anything.

They would still have my back.

12

When no one looked differently at me when I went back to work, I shook off the fact that Sara knew. I went back to making sure I was putting all that I learned to practice. Only now, I wasn't under the tutelage of a drill sergeant of a nurse. I was in neurology now, and it was a little less stressful, so my days seemed easier.

Well, as easier as residency could get.

I was able to have lunch with Bryce on some days. Surprisingly, he didn't push the boundary of just friends. He didn't act like the doting boyfriend. He sat on the opposite side of the table, and we chatted about normal things. The only difference was when we parted ways.

He didn't give me the usual kiss on the cheek. He gave me a peck on the lips, and something in his eyes sparked something in my chest. The rush had me smiling lightly at him as I went back to work.

This was something I could do.

When it came to our usual meet up, I got the same feeling. The only difference was we weren't entertaining one of Bryce's girls of the moment. I guess that made me his girl of the moment, but I didn't get the same treatment. I didn't get handed cash and a command for beer, I wasn't ignored.

None of them treated me like I was anything different. It was oddly a relief. I didn't know if I could handle one of them going all possessive boyfriend on me. There was no throwback to the feeling Kenny gave me. It was normalcy with a little more feelings involved.

I got kisses from each of them when we went to leave the bar without any sort of ordeal. If we got looks from other people, I didn't notice. I was to the point now that I didn't care.

I didn't think. I just kept on and enjoyed every bit of affection they gave me. The sex, something I experimented with each of them, was explosive. Bryce kept his word, taking me home and showing me that he wasn't so quick to bust. He made time to twist me into positions that made my toes curl and left me gasping with the relief of it.

As a group, sex was amazing, but one on one, it was just as good. It was more than just sex. Whether I was with all of them or just one of them.

When he finished, Bryce wrapped me up in his arms and held me. I felt the heavy thump of his heart against my cheek and the flare of a connection between us. The fact we were able to do this in my bed, my room, just added to it.

"I love you," I whispered to him. I'd said it before in a room where they were all there. But I hadn't tried saying it to any of them while we were one on one.

There was a stretch of silence between us, and this was the first time I considered that their feelings might be different from mine. I didn't want to be expectant, but I was hoping he wouldn't leave me hanging. Now that I thought back to it, none of them had returned the sentiment. Panic caught up in my throat, and I tried not to let it show on my face.

Bryce cupped my face, his thumb skimming over my cheekbone. His lips brushed mine, and my panic ebbed away. I relaxed back against him and decided I didn't need to hear it. I could just take the affection he offered.

"I don't think there's ever been a time where I haven't loved you," he murmured low. His lips were against my brow. "You've had to know that. There's no way we could've been grown up together and been friends for this long without me loving you."

I wrapped my arms around his middle and hugged him tightly. That was the reassurance I needed. Something I would go on to look for with Noah, who said something similar.

***

"I've waited for this opportunity for so long," he said lightly. "I was afraid of the day where you'd find a man who would replace us. I guess you were running into the same problem." Noah smiled over his cup of coffee on one of the days where he picked me up for breakfast—and something more—before I went from the night shift back to mornings. While I enjoyed his bed, I was just as eager to have him in mine. "You were trying to find someone that fit an ideal, and no one would ever measure up." He looked away as he said it. It sounded like the beginning of what Bryce had said that rolled us into what we were doing now.

"It wasn't a matter of them not measuring up," I admitted as I looked at my hands. "It's what they wanted me to give up. I couldn't cut you guys lose for the sake of a guy who I wasn't sure would be around more than six months." I grimaced and twisted my fingers together. "I figured if there was a right guy for me, he'd be able to find a happy medium where I kept you guys in the picture."

"It's funny how this worked out then," Noah hummed as he took up one of my hands. "Now you're with three men who aren't at all jealous of your relationship with your friends." I looked up to see his grin as he brushed his lips against my knuckles. "Pretty lucky situation you got yourself into."

I snorted in agreement, then considered my next words carefully. "Bryce told me he loved me," I said gently.

"Well, yeah." Noah didn't look at all surprised. "Dude has probably been crushing on you since we all first met." He leaned closer and prodded me, "How does that make you feel?"

I smiled at him. "Happy. I told him I loved him. I told you all how I feel." I raised an eyebrow at him. "Now it's just a matter of figuring you out."

"Figuring me out?" He looked confused for a moment, resting back against his pillow and headboard. "I thought I was obvious."

"Sometimes I can be oblivious," I offered to him. Besides it being the truth, it was hard to admit. But after facing what had brought us this far, I'd be 'gracious' in this moment.

"I've loved you since you first started noticing other guys." He drew closer to me. "I remember your first boyfriend and wanting to beat the snot out of him when I knew he had kissed you." He shrugged a little, still close. "I hated the idea of sharing you with anyone else, but I am okay with Bryce and Lucas."

"Bryce was my first kiss." I leaned forward to brush my lips against his.

He had a moment of confusion. "When? I thought it was Jacob Hawkins."

I shook my head. While Jacob had asked me out, I never considered him a boyfriend. I wouldn't say that aloud. There'd been something to that, a boy claiming me when I thought I was otherwise invisible to anyone but my boys.

"Maybe he was just trying to make you jealous. And Casey Dawson's party. Right when we hit high school."

He laughed then. "I remember that. We'd thought for sure that when he disappeared, you'd killed him and buried him in her backyard." Noah looked amused still and pulled away. "It's fitting. One of us got to be your first kiss. I'd be lying if I said I wasn't jealous. But it's the way it should've been." He wrapped an arm around me then. "There's another first time that should've been one of ours."

I settled against him. "I don't know that things would've worked out the way that they have if I'd slept with you first instead of Derek." I kissed his chest and smiled to myself. "I think I had to see what was out there before I realized where I belonged."

"Yeah," he murmured, his fingers finding my chin. When I looked up at him, I saw a swirl of emotion in his dark eyes. "I love you." It came out of him in a breath, and I felt my heart twist into a knot.

I leaned forward to kiss him, another one of my boys telling me what I needed to hear. Even if I knew it all along, it felt good to hear it though.

Bryce and Noah both showed me that I could bring my boys home without consequence. Well, I wasn't brave enough to have all three of them here, but I hungered for another moment. The only one I hadn't had a moment with was Lucas. While I saw him at each of our gatherings, I didn't get the chance to bring him home like I very much wanted to.

But Lucas had excuses. "After the last time we came back to my place, I figured I should put it back together. That way I don't have to worry about someone stepping on a nail or a tack," he said over his beer at our bar. "I wasn't in a hurry to finish up the house before because I rarely had visitors. It was just a project to keep me entertained."

"You don't have to hurry up and finish it," I told him. "I mean, I got my place, and Noah has his. There are still options."

"I'm okay with having my hands full," he assured me. "Just worry about me when I'm done." He leaned close to me. "Then you'll have to give me something to do when I have more free time."

It felt like a dodge to me. I wouldn't get him to come home with me and have him in my bed. If I wanted the opportunity with Lucas to make sure he understood how I felt, I had to go to him. Now, it was a matter of finding the time and a chance to do that.

13

I was arrogant, and I didn't realize that until I came home one evening from work. I felt mentally drained and damn near zombified when I ran into Sara. She looked like she was expecting me, and she had her arms folded over her chest. I was too tired to figure it out, so I stood in the doorway, waiting for her to tell me what's up.

There was smugness on her face that dwindled when she realized I wasn't on the same page. She shoved a folded piece of paper into my face. "Rent and utilities are late," she said with a smirk, but I could see the disappointment in her face.

Her words didn't clear up my confusion though. I unfolded the paper and looked at a written, itemized bill. There was my half of the rent, the power, and water bills halved. It was neat, and as far as I could tell, she wasn't trying to rob me. Then I saw the 'late fee' labeled down at the bottom of the paper.

Two hundred dollars on top of the rent and utilities.

"It was due on the first," she went on like I wasn't standing there looking at the bill. "You're a week late. I'm giving you another week to pay it, or I'm going to evict you."

I blinked at her, not connecting it just yet. "She didn't pay you?"

"Nope." Sara gave something that might've been pity if there wasn't so much bitch mixed in with it. She turned away from me to sit on the couch. "Must've pissed off Mommy," she said in such a condescending manner, it was an effort to not throw her attitude back at her.

I turned and went down the hallway to my bedroom. I pulled my phone out and had Mama's number queued up before I stalled. I wanted an explanation from her. After all, we had an agreement. But what if something was wrong? It'd been too long since I called her. I thumbed up Lucas' number next and waited, counting slowly to ten to calm myself down. I didn't need to panic, yet.

Everything was fine; Mama was fine. She was probably just mad that I was ignoring her. Sure, she'd never done anything like that before, but that didn't mean anything.

Lucas picked up on the third ring. "What's up, Buttercup?"

"Can I get you to do me a favor?" I asked hurriedly, the memory of him after his mom died playing in my mind's eye. He was wrecked after he found her collapsed in her bedroom; it was part of the reason he stripped the entire house.

I didn't know what I would do if I called her, and she didn't answer the phone.

"Sure." He cleared his throat. "Though if it's anything sexual, I should point out that I've been laying tile all day, and I'm a sweaty mess. My back fucking hurts, and you'd probably have to do all the work." He kind of sounded nervous, like he wasn't ready for it to be that. But he probably wouldn't tell me no.

"No," I said quickly. "No, it's not that." I took a breath, "Mama didn't pay rent like she usually does. I was hoping you'd go check on her for me?"

He was quiet for a beat, and I heard the front door open. "The front porch light is on like usual," he reported, and I heard him puff a little as he crossed the street. "So is the light in the front room." He paused, "I don't have a shirt on. If she lectures me, I'm gonna give her the phone."

"You're my hero," I mumbled into the phone. "My savior. I would sacrifice furry animals in your name, but the squirrels by my apartment are big and mean. I don't think I could take them."

He snorted a laugh but didn't comment. I heard his heavy hand on the front door as he spoke quietly to me, "I can't see her in the front room."

The grip on my phone tightened to the point I felt the plastic case bite into my palm. "There's a spare key under a rock in her garden," I said impatiently. "If she doesn't answer the door, can you—"

"Frankie," he cut me off, and I heard the distinct noise of the front door opening. There was always the sound of a seal breaking and the squeak of hinges.

"What are you doing here?" Mama's voice sounded cold; it was how she talked to my friends. She never liked them, so she was never polite to them.

"Mrs. Moore," he said by way of a greeting. "Frankie. She was worried about you. She asked me to come over and make sure you were okay," Lucas said gently. At some point, he must've put me on speakerphone because I heard the rustle of the wind.

"She still has a phone," Mama snapped. "She is perfectly capable of calling me on her own. I realize she has been too busy with you miscreants, whoring herself out to the three of you. But I am still her mother, and she can face me. You can tell her that for me."

My heart fell into my stomach, and I sat heavily on my bed. Mama knew. She didn't pay my rent like she usually did because she knew. She knew, and she was mad enough to let me go homeless.

"I will," Lucas' voice came over the line. "I'm on the way to pick you up." Then he ended the call.

I stayed in my bed, trying to figure out the best route of action now. I had been saving my paychecks for the last few months, and I was perfectly able to pay my own rent. It would put me behind on my plans, but if Mama had decided to cut me off—I choked on my breath at just the idea.

There were moments in my life where I thought I'd disappointed my mother. There were a lot of cold glares I had received growing up. A lot of comments that had me wondering what I did wrong. Being a teenager, if I had gotten mouthy with her, it only took one look from her to have me apologizing and sending myself to my room.

Now? I wasn't sure what to do. I was cowed before even talking to her.

When my bedroom door opened, I saw Lucas. His hair was a disheveled mess, and he still wore the kneepads he'd had on while laying tile. He hadn't even bothered to pull on a shirt between knocking on Mama's front door and coming to me.

"C'mon," he said gently, offering me a hand.

I took his hand and let him lead me out of the apartment I shared with Sara. She was still on the couch and didn't even give us a second look. There were no smart remarks about not paying rent, no appreciative comments about Lucas not having a shirt.

Lucas didn't give her a second look either. He held onto my hand with a vise-like grip as he tugged me down the steps to his battered pickup truck. He opened the passenger door for me and helped me in before he went around the front.

The ride to Mama's was silent. I didn't know what exactly was going through his head, but it felt like it was eating at him. Almost as much as the situation I created with my mother was devouring me.

"What do I do?" I asked when he pulled into the neighborhood we all lived in as kids. Seeing the house had my heart in my throat. I wasn't twenty-four anymore. I was back to being twelve when Mama caught Lucas outside my window.

"Well," he released a breath. "Tell her the truth. She probably doesn't know all the details and is assuming something."

"If she's assuming something…." I started. "Then I can make something up, and I don't need to tell her the truth. I can just make her think what's going on isn't what's going on."

"Tell her the truth." His voice hardened. "Dancing around lies won't make this easier. She's not going to trust your word unless you give her the truth." He gave me a look as he pulled to a stop in front of her house. "Lying to her means you're going to spend the rest of your life lying. Is that what you want to do?"

"I don't," I answered honestly.

"Then tell her the truth," he said gently. "I'll be right behind you no matter what." As if to emphasize his point, he sat with me in his truck, waiting for me to make the first move.

I counted my heartbeats as I tried to figure out if there was any possible way to do this without everything falling apart on me. *I could have everything, right? It was possible for me to find a happy medium between my boys and my mom, right?* I could do this without cracking. I could do this without giving up everything I wanted.

"You can do this," Lucas added like he could hear my panic. He took up my hand again and held onto it tightly. "I'm right here with you."

I nodded shakily and opened the door. I let go of his hand and turned to get out of his truck. I looked up at the front door, half-expecting Mama to be there, glaring at me. All I saw was the closed door. I crossed the well-manicured lawn and had my keys in my hand. I could just open the door and confront her, which would be the brave thing to do. I could tell her that I wasn't a whore, and the relationship I had with my boys might not be conventional, but I was happy.

Instead, I knocked.

I felt Lucas behind me, but I didn't dare look at him. I didn't want to see any of his judgment. But the fact he was there was enough to keep me from turning around to run back to his truck.

Mama opened the door, and her face was the cold mask I'd seen before. She didn't open the door wide enough to invite me in. She just stood in the doorway with her hands folded in front of her apron and her back straight. "Francine," her voice was hard. "I almost didn't recognize you. It's been so long," she murmured as if to overshadow the fact she was so angry with me, it was just disappointment.

"Residency, Mama," I started like I didn't know this would be a catastrophic conversation. "I'm usually so tired when I come home, I go right to bed."

Mama's eyes narrowed, and I knew she didn't believe me. "Excuses are all well and good, Francine," she said evenly. "But we both know that's all they are. Excuses. I've given you the best years of my life. I've worked hard to keep a roof over your head and make sure you went through school with no distractions. Save the distraction I couldn't get you to let go of." She looked over my shoulder for a beat. "I always knew this would happen. That you three would lead her down the path of perversity."

"They didn't lead me anywhere," I objected.

"I didn't raise a whore," she snapped at me, her voice rising to a point that I jumped a little. "You were supposed to save yourself for marriage. You made a promise that you would wait." Her voice quivered for a moment. "I raised you to do that."

"I never planned on getting married," I said gently. "I didn't when I made that promise, and I still don't want to." I waved a hand behind me. "That's not their fault. This…" I took a breath. "This is my decision to be with all three of them. They didn't talk me into it, the decision was mine. It was a decision I made without their interference. I made this choice," I continued in the face of her growing distaste, "because I love them. All three of them."

"It's immoral," she bit back at me. "Shameful and sinful. I won't encourage it, and I won't continue to pay for you to live a lifestyle I don't approve of. You can try to blame the failed relationship your father and I had on your poor choices." The only emotional reaction she seemed to have was then. Her chin quivered, but her eyes narrowed. "But you didn't grow up with neither your father nor I flaunting anything close to this abomination."

"Mama." I took a step closer, knowing if I could get her to listen to me, I could get her to understand. "It's not what you think it is. It's nothing like that." Lucas grabbed my hand, holding it tightly. I couldn't tell if he were trying to give me support or hold me back. I didn't bother to tug away from his grasp. "Please," I couldn't hold myself together anymore, "Mama. Just try to understand. I'm not a whore. I'm not sleeping around."

"I don't want to hear it," she snapped at me again. "I don't want to hear about your perversities." Mama took a step back into the house, her expression schooled into that cold mask I was familiar with. "If this is the route you intend to go down, then you are free to experience the consequences of it. Pay your own rent, pay your own bills. See what it's truly like to be an adult."

"This isn't about money." I struggled for a moment to get my emotions under control. "This would have never been about money."

"Well then." She reached behind her to tighten the sash of her apron. "I will see you when you're done being a whore." She gave me a final look before she closed the door.

14

Seven years old

I could hear Mama and Daddy yelling, even though the door to their bedroom was closed. I couldn't understand what they were saying, but I knew Mama was crying. I could hear it in her voice. She didn't cry often, and it could only mean that something was wrong.

I stayed in the living room like Daddy had asked me to. The television was on, and he had turned the volume up louder than Mama would've liked, so I turned it down. That's when I heard them yelling. I didn't pay the cartoons any mind. I stood in front of the couch, looking back at their bedroom door.

I didn't know what I was supposed to do. I knew when Daddy sat me down, he just told me to watch TV, that he and Mama wouldn't be long. But one cartoon was over, and another started, and they were still yelling.

I knew it wasn't good that they were yelling at one another like this. I knew that when my friends yelled at one another, a teacher usually stepped in. I didn't think I could do that. I didn't want them to yell at me.

The door flew open, and I jumped, hoping that everything would be okay now that they were done. Usually, after they were done fighting, everything would be okay. It wasn't the first time they fought; maybe it would end like all the other times.

"If you leave..." Mama was still in the bedroom, but I couldn't see her. It sounded like she was crying. "I don't ever want to see you again." My heart jumped into my throat, and I looked at Daddy. "You don't get to come back from this, Joseph."

He stood in the living room with me; his gray hair was disheveled and the button down he wore was wrinkled. He didn't look like he had just come home from work. He looked like he and Mama had got into a fistfight. I bit my lip because I could feel my chin quiver. He had a bag in his hand.

"Daddy, where are you going?" I asked. If he left, he wouldn't be able to come back.

"Ladybug…" His voice was hoarse, and he looked like he was about to cry. Daddy didn't cry, and I felt tears coming to my eyes in response. "Daddy is going to leave. I want you to know, that no matter what your mother tells you, I love you." He pressed a kiss to my forehead.

"Daddy?" I whined when he stepped away from me. "Daddy, don't go. Please."

He didn't act as if he heard me. He stood and walked out the door like I hadn't said anything. I quaked, tears streaming down my cheeks because I didn't know what to do. What could I have done to stop him? I went to the door after him, opening it to see him already in his car, pulling out of the driveway.

"Daddy!" I started down the steps of the front porch. "Take me with you, please!"

By the time I got to the road, I felt a pair of arms come around my middle. Mama held me tight despite the fact I screamed for Daddy.

"Let him go." Her voice was in my ear. "Let him go be with his whore. We aren't good enough for him anymore." She didn't sound upset about it. She just sounded angry.

I stopped fighting her and just let her hold me as I cried. I didn't know what a whore was, but if Daddy was leaving me for one, then I knew it was bad. A whore was what broke up my family.

15

Present Day

I didn't remember how I got into Lucas' bed, but I assumed he had carried me home. I was wrapped up in the smell of him, and it was far more comforting than anything else in the world. This right here, leaning up against the wall with his pillows propped up on either side of me, was more like home than what was across the street. That alone was probably keeping me from cracking.

My phone was blowing up beside me, but I hadn't had the nerve to look at it. Mama didn't reach out before, she wouldn't reach out now. That meant the only other people who were reaching out were Noah and Bryce. That meant that Lucas had told them what happened.

It must have been something he did between putting me in his bed and jumping in the shower, where he was now. I should feel grateful that he'd pulled me off Mama's front porch, before I got the attention of the entire neighborhood. But something irrational sat in my gut.

He told me to tell her the truth. What good had that done me? She didn't want anything to do with me now. I would've been much better off cooking up some sort of lie and playing it off like she was assuming the worst. Technically, I didn't have a boyfriend. The boys were just my friends and nothing more. It would've been so much easier to lie than to face all that disappointment she threw at me.

The water in the bathroom cut off. Anger boiled in me, and I knew it was misplaced. But I wanted to blame him. I wanted to do it so badly, I could taste it.

He doesn't deserve it.

Lucas came out of the bathroom with a towel around his waist. He didn't give me a second glance as he went to the dresser for clothes. He dropped the towel from his waist, giving me a good view of his naked form. Anger quickly turned into something else, and I was up off the bed before he had the chance to pull his boxer shorts on.

I kissed his shoulder, tasting the dampness that still clung to him. I wound an arm around his middle and tipped up on my toes so I could follow the line of his shoulder to his neck. I heard him swallow as I traced the path with my tongue and kissed the strong column of his throat. I pressed against his back and pressed my hand against his chest, feeling the heavy thump of his heart.

I could use this. I could use the distraction, and I wanted him so much. My hand drifted down from his chest, tracing the line of his abdomen until I felt the little line of pubic hair that led me right down where I wanted. I heard his breath catch as my fingers found their way around the base of his cock. His erection was already at half mast, and it probably wouldn't take much effort to get him hard enough for this.

I started to stroke him with all the intention of tugging him to the bed and finally getting a moment with him that I'd been craving. He made a noise deep in his throat, then caught my wrist. "We don't need to do this."

"I want this," I said against his neck. "I want you."

"Trust me when I say I want you, too." He pulled my hand from his cock and turned to me as he said it. "But doing this now won't make you feel better."

"My mother just cut me off," I snapped at him. "I need to feel a connection with someone I love. How will that not make me feel better?"

"Because she called you a whore," he said gently, holding onto my shoulders now. "If we do this now, all you'll do is feel like she was right. And she's not. But if we do this, all you're going to do is regret it." He cupped my face in his hands then, holding me in place when all I wanted to do was pull away from him. "I will not fuck you if all you're going to do is regret it. Do you understand me?"

"How is she wrong?" I wobbled on the edge, the lust and anger twisting up in my gut so much, it weighed down to my knees. "How is she wrong?" I sniffled again. "There's nothing normal about what we're doing."

"How many people have you been with?" He kept his grip on me firm, holding me up and keeping me close. "What? Ten? Twelve?"

"Counting the three of you, eight," I answered honestly.

Lucas smiled weakly at me. "That's what I figured. Being with the three of us doesn't make you a whore. That's not what a whore is."

"But…" I started to protest.

He cut me off with a well-placed kiss, swallowing any argument I had. When he pulled away, he spoke before I got the opportunity, "Your mom said what she knew would hurt you because she was hurt too. She doesn't understand. That's all it is." He pressed his brow to mine. "You are not a whore."

"She's never going to understand," I murmured as I closed my eyes. "It's not normal to her, so that instantly makes it wrong. As long as we do this, she's going to hate me for it."

His hands slipped away from my face, and I opened my eyes to meet his. There was something somber to his blue depths, and I knew what he would say before he even opened his mouth. I already shook my head.

"We can put an end to this then," he said it anyway, as a statement... Like it was even an option. "We go back to being just friends."

"We can't go back to being friends," I snapped at him. "I can't forget any of this, and I know damn well Noah and Bryce can't either."

"Tough shit," he said, like it wasn't a big deal.

"Maybe I don't want to go backward," I said angrily. "If it's not obvious, I was a willing participant in everything we did. Better yet, I'm positive this was my idea."

"I don't want to go backward either, Frank." He stepped away from me so he could tug his boxers on. "But family is important." He looked at me hard. "Trust me, I realize the significance to it. I don't have it anymore."

A pounding at his front door interrupted our conversation, followed by the death rattle buzz of his doorbell. I was sure Mama saw him take me to his house. Was she here to give me a bigger piece of her mind? I didn't think I could handle another reaming from her, but I headed out of his bedroom before he could stop me.

"Nope." He grabbed my shoulder. "Wait here. I'll handle it." He had a pair of basketball shorts on before he managed to intercept me. He had a t-shirt in hand and only paused to tug it on before he went to the front door.

I stayed in the hallway and took note of the fact he had taken the tile from his bedroom through the rest of the house. It was all the way down the hallway, and from what I could see, he had it in the living room. I stepped into the next doorway down from the master bedroom. The tile was in there, too. The grout was a dark color that blended seamlessly with the tile texture. It looked like real hardwood. Looking at the spare room, the only thing it needed was to be painted. I didn't pay attention to who was at the front door now. Instead, I went to the next bedroom to see it in a similar state. Then I found the guest bathroom, and it was still half-finished. The tub, toilet, and sink were in, but it was obvious when I had called him earlier, he'd been in here working. The tile work in here was similar to what he had in the master bath with clean, crisp lines that impressed me. The amount of patience he had was impressive.

Looking at the work he'd done distracted me from who our visitors were. But I was close enough to the living room, I could hear Mrs. Kemp's voice.

"What the hell is that lady going on about?" Her question had all the fire and attitude I knew her for. "Why is she accusing you and Noah of corrupting her daughter?"

"I got the same phone call," Mrs. Wilks said in a similar tone of voice without the ass-kicking attitude that Mrs. Kemp carried. "I haven't been able to get him to answer his phone."

"They didn't corrupt me," I answered for Lucas. He, for the most part, looked flustered in front of the two moms. "It was my idea, so it's my fault. They didn't do anything."

Both women looked at me surprised. Lucas gave me an irritated look; he hadn't wanted me to be a part of this conversation. Well, if the truth was good for my mama, it would be good for Noah and Bryce's, too.

"Frankie…" Mrs. Wilks looked concerned as she stepped further into Lucas' living room. "Your mother called us both upset. Is everything okay?" The fact she didn't ask for clarification made me love her so much.

I felt my throat burn as tears threatened. This woman always had a way of making my control over my emotions weak. "Mama's angry with me, and she's blaming them." I waved a hand towards Lucas. "I tried to tell her it was all my idea, but she wouldn't have it."

"Well, what happened to make her come to that conclusion?" Mrs. Kemp snapped. "If I need to beat Noah's ass, don't you try to keep it from happening. You might as well be one of my own. So, if this is something serious, I need to know." She had a hand on her hip, eyeing me like she already knew she could take me if she needed to.

I floundered for a minute, trying to decide if I should go with the truth or let Noah and Bryce break it to their moms. Lucas decided for me. "We moved to the next step."

"What does that mean?" Mrs. Wilks asked, giving me a final worried look before she turned back to Lucas.

Mrs. Kemp, on the other hand, put a hand to her chest and looked at Lucas. "You asked her to marry you? I always knew it would be one of you boys, but… I guess I always assumed it would be Noah."

Mrs. Wilks pulled her phone from the pocket of her Bermuda shorts. "I thought it might be my Bryce," she murmured.

"I didn't ask her to marry me." Lucas made a face, probably after listening to my mother. "We all moved to the next step."

"All of you," Mrs. Wilks echoed as she looked back to me.

"It was my idea," I said weakly.

"Well…" Mrs. Kemp looked at me, too, with surprise evident on her face. "I guess that makes things easier between the four of you." Her lips twisted up, then she snorted. "Now I see why the tight-assed old lady was so angry. This is fine." She shrugged her shoulders. "You've been taking care of each other this long, we shouldn't be surprised it went this route."

"Does this mean I'm not going to get grandbabies?" Mrs. Wilks came to me as she asked it, her brown eyes huge. "Don't tell me this means I don't get to be a grandma."

I saw Lucas' ears go red, and before I could even comment on it, he stepped in. "That's—we haven't even talked about it, Linda. We're still figuring out the mechanics to it. Kids and all of that isn't something that'll happen right now. Probably not even in the near future."

"Boy…" Mrs. Kemp grabbed onto his arm with a death-grip pinch I'd been fortunate enough to have only heard about. "Don't you tell me you're not giving me grandbabies."

Lucas buckled, leaning down as he struggled to not jerk his arm away from her. "That's not up to me," he gritted out. "I wouldn't say no to it, I swear! Please let go!" Once she did, he rubbed the under part of his arm. "This is like way too early to be talking about this. Besides, this isn't something that's just up to me. She," he pointed at me, "has the deciding factor on all of that."

"Are you sicking them on me?" I asked because both women looked at me.

"No," Mrs. Kemp answered for him with a chuckle. "But it does answer a few things for me." She looked at Bryce's mom. "We still got time, hunny. She ain't closed up shop on us, yet." She smiled, and if it weren't for the fact her face was rounder, I would've seen Noah in her smile. "Girl, your mama is upset about it. I see why. But I'm not going to butt into your business like that. What matters to me is that my child is happy." She released a breath and closed the distance before I could protest. She wrapped me up in a hug I couldn't resist. I melted in her arms and took her comfort. "If this makes you happy, and you can handle all three of them, then that's all that matters."

"It's not normal," Bryce's mom said from beside us. "It's not something everyone will readily accept. But that's not what's important." Her voice was gentle compared to the attitude that Noah's mom had. "What other people think isn't important. You of all people should know that. Were you happy before you started this arrangement with the boys?"

I stepped away from Mrs. Kemp to consider it. To think about what she was asking. "Happy isn't a word I would use," I answered truthfully. I shrugged a little as I tried to not over-analyze myself. "I was functioning."

Both of the older women looked at me, eyeing me carefully. What did they see?

"Up until today," Mrs. Wilks began. "Were you happy?"

I opened my mouth, the first word that came to mind was yes. A vehement yes.

"The only times I can ever say I'm happy is when I'm with one of them or all of them," I admitted. "They're the only people who know me and support me. Except for Mama." My breath caught. "She supported me financially. She made sure I had a roof over my head and that I ate. She made sure my bills were paid."

"So, basically you're saying, she did all the adult things for you?" Mrs. Kemp raised an eyebrow at me. "Girl," she frowned at me, "at some point in your life, you have to leave your mother's shadow. With her paying for everything, you're allowing her to have control over you and your choices. Now you need to decide which is more important." She tilted her head as she eyed me. "Having your mother's approval or being happy?"

"I can't believe you would encourage her," Lucas protested. "You're encouraging her to be with three men. Are you just doing this to spite Mrs. Moore?"

"Patricia has never been a friend of mine," Mrs. Kemp snapped. "The only time she gave me and my son any ounce of respect was when she found out that one boy was spreading foul rumors about Frankie. She didn't find out about that until after she demanded I keep Noah away from her when he was suspended." She shot a glare at Lucas. "You know what I'm talking about, don't you?"

He nodded, fidgeting under the weight of her glare.

"I would never encourage any of you to do anything I thought was dangerous. But tell me one thing that's dangerous about this situation?" She paused and raised a hand. "One of you want to put a ring on it? Make it official and the other two get jealous?"

"She gets pregnant, and we don't know who the father is until a test can be done?" Mrs. Wilks piped up. "Though, that wouldn't upset me much. Honestly, it wouldn't matter who the father was to me because I would still be able to be a grandma regardless." She grinned at me. "I laid claim to you from the moment he first brought you into my house. I would spoil any baby you had regardless of if it was related to me by blood."

"She said she didn't want to get married," Lucas spoke up again. "Honestly, the only person I ever considered for that role was her. But I know why she doesn't want to, so it wouldn't be an issue."

"Jealousy is probably the only issue they have here," Mrs. Kemp said. "And if you've gotten this far, you've managed to figure out something." She waved both hands. "You both might as well be my kids. I don't want to know the details of what you do. Just don't get arrested. Be happy, that's all I ask for from Noah."

I sniffled, the need to cry so much more now. I dissolved, crumbling to my knees on the floor. My mother would never be like my friends' mothers. There'd be no acceptance of this. There'd be no worrying about whether

I was happy. I doubted that there was ever an occasion where she had questioned my mental health.

What am I supposed to do?

"Girl, get up," Mrs. Kemp snapped at me, suddenly a drill sergeant. "It's time to grow up. Learn what it takes to be an adult. Snap together and pay your bills yourself. You haven't needed your mom for years. You shouldn't need to fall apart now." She had her hands under my armpits and heaved me up. "Show her you're okay. That you're going to make it. That what she wants out of you she won't get. Then I promise you, she'll decide that she still wants you as a daughter, even if she disagrees with what you're doing."

"Lucas has been without his mother for a few years now," Mrs. Wilks added gently. "You'll make it. You have the benefit of knowing she's still alive." She rubbed my back while the woman in front of me tried to toughen me up. Bryce's mom was trying to soothe me. "It'll be okay. You're strong enough to handle this."

I nodded. "I am." I hiccupped. "I can be an adult. I'll be okay."

"Good." Mrs. Kemp kissed my cheek. "Now I'm gonna leave you two to talk. You might want to call the other boys here, too. This is the one free pass I'll give you for breaking Noah's heart if you decide you'd rather do what your mother wants." She turned away and looked at Lucas. "Unless you can talk her out of doing that. If that happens, then there are no free passes."

"You know we love you no matter what." Mrs. Wilks pressed a kiss to my cheek. "If you need me, I'm just a phone call away."

They left then, seemingly satisfied with what they'd learned. It did cement the fact that I wasn't alone, even if Mama had cut me off. I just needed to decide if I wanted to accept that I was cut off and keep going, or if I wanted to leave my boys and go back to Mama. I leaned against the unpainted wall and looked at him.

"What do you want to do now?" Lucas asked as he lingered by his front door.

"I want to go to bed and sleep." I rubbed a hand over my face. "I've got to work tomorrow, and I need to figure out what I need to do to grow up."

"C'mon." He stepped around me and led the way back to his bedroom. "I've got this adulting crap figured out. I'll show you how I do it."

16

I decided after a long day of work that the best thing I could think to do with my situation was to carry on as usual. I hadn't paid my rent, yet, but I was toying with the idea of moving out. I figured out Mama had found out about the boys and me one of two ways.

She could've been peeking in Lucas' windows; the lack of blinds would have easily exposed us that first night we made the decision to go down this rabbit hole. We had given the pizza man an eyeful after all. If she'd been out in the yard doing work, then it would be completely understandable if she had seen Bryce or Noah kiss me.

But was she even outside then? I couldn't recall. It didn't seem likely. It was dusk, and Mama was a creature of habit when it came to an early dinner.

The other option, the more likely of options, was Sara. My roommate was always glued to her phone. I never thought much about it before. People were glued to their phones. Mama had a cell phone, so there was a good chance they could've been communicating.

Mama had picked out the apartment for me, something she had insisted on. She didn't want me living with one of the boys, something that had been offered. She knew Sara, though I couldn't think of anytime outside of that first meeting where I saw the two of them talking.

But that didn't mean she couldn't have been calling her on the phone. This theory seemed more plausible to me. After all, if Mama had seen anything that first night, I would've felt the consequences a whole lot sooner.

I walked in the door and still had that thought in the back of my mind when I saw her on the couch.

"Rent's still due," she said around a mouthful of my popcorn. "If you make me wait another week, I'm gonna add another hundred bucks to it."

I'd almost forgotten about it. I stood by the front door, tempted to turn around and walk out, when it occurred to me now was as good a time as any to ask. I looked at Sara as she thumbed through her phone, and the television blared a commercial I was unfamiliar with.

"Did you tell my mother?" I asked her.

"Tell your mom what?" She didn't even look at me. It looked like she was striving for something so she wouldn't have to. Her eyes flicked from her phone to the television, and she stuffed another handful of popcorn into her mouth.

"Did you tell my mom that you thought I was sleeping with my friends?" I clarified with a growing amount of irritation.

"Thought?" She snorted and finally looked at me. "Girl, who are you kidding? You're fucking all three of those guys." She looked back at the television and curled a lip. "Always thought you were greedy."

I glared at her now. "So, you told my mom that I was sleeping with all three of them? You're so jealous, you'd rat me out to my mom?"

She gave me a look this time with a smugness that had my stomach knotting up. "She wanted tabs. I gave her tabs. I told her when one of your dudes stayed the night and where they slept. When they stopped sleeping on the couch, it was obvious." She looked back down at her phone. "Not my fault she got mad at you. You have to own up to what you do, Frannie."

"Thanks," I said sarcastically and turned to open the front door again. I had my phone out as I made my way down to the ATM. This was the final nail in the coffin. The first number I dialed was Bryce. He answered on the second ring. "Are there any units available in your building?" I asked in lieu of a greeting.

"Um," I heard a rustle, "I don't know. Why do you ask? Does this have something to do with my mom calling me about us?"

"Kind of." I gave a cursory look around the ATM before I pulled the rent Sara demanded from my account. "Sara told my mom about all of us," I snipped into the phone. "I'm not going to live here anymore so she can keep reporting back to Mama."

"I'm all for you getting out." It sounded like he perked up. "I mean… I'd offer you a room at my place, but well… I went cheap and got a studio apartment. Noah's got a pretty big place. He's not that far from the hospital. If you get desperate, you can move in with Lucas. He's got plenty of room in his house."

"You're offering the other guys' places without asking them?" I asked as I stuffed the money into my purse and began that paranoid power walk back to the apartment. "Don't you think Lucas and Noah should have a say in that?"

"Well, obviously, they have the final say. But if you're living with one of them, there's less of a chance that you end up moving in with another creeper." He made a noise. "No dude roommates unless it's one of us. Not that

I don't trust you," he started quickly. "I trust you. Just other dudes... I don't trust them."

"Don't worry, Dad," I said sarcastically as I let myself back into the apartment. "I'll make sure I find a place you approve of."

"I thought I'd like it if you called me Daddy, but it's just weird, Frankie," he complained.

"Whatever. Gimme a sec." I pulled the phone from my ear and dug the money from my purse. Sara was still parked on the couch, so there was no point in trying to dodge her or to drag this out any further. I offered her the bundle of twenties. "Consider this my notice that I'm going to be vacating at the end of the month, and thanks for making it so I had to carry around an uncomfortable amount of money to make sure you got paid."

"Your mom always direct deposited it in my account," she shot back. "How was I supposed to know you wouldn't be smart enough to do that?"

"Probably the same way you would be smart enough to realize I wouldn't know you got my rent until you waited a week to tell me," I snapped before deciding against humoring her. "But hey, thanks for eating my food. Really appreciate it." I turned to head to my room, putting my phone back to my ear. "I can count on you to help me pack, right?"

"Count me in!" He sounded excited. "Let's figure out where you're planning on crashing first. Then you can pay me in pizza, beer, and sex to get you moved."

"All three? I don't think I have that much stuff." I sat on my bed as I spoke to him. "I feel like you're asking too much here, B. Let me get a new place first."

"Who am I kidding? You can just pay me in sex. I'll lift all the heavy things, no complaints."

17

"My apartment is too small. I know we wouldn't be able to fit all her stuff there." Bryce was a little louder the more beer he drank. "Plus, if you hit it from the right spot, she gets loud," he said like he was divulging some sort of secret to the other two men. "We wouldn't be able to live there long before she got us evicted." He dropped a shot glass on the table we were crowded around. "Otherwise, I'd stash her there no problem."

"I signed a new lease three months ago." Noah pulled a face. "Before we started all this. If I saw this being a problem, I would've waited so I could look into getting something bigger. I mean, she can fit there no problem, but it's a one bedroom." He looked at me, and there was something timid about his face. "Moving in wouldn't be a problem. It makes it seem like there's some stability to this. Like it's a committed relationship."

"Isn't that what it is?" Lucas asked. "You're not seeing someone on the side, are you?"

"No," Noah answered.

Which was quickly followed by Bryce's, "Hell no. Do you have any idea how much I've wanted this? And for how long? Shit." He was slurring a little, and I glanced at a nearby table to see if they were following our conversation. "Haven't looked at another chick since we started this."

"I guess that's comforting to hear," I spoke up. "But I don't necessarily need to move in with one of you guys. I should be able to get a place of my own. I just…" I paused, looking down at the table. "Mama always did these things for me. I let her. I didn't try to be independent. All I'm looking for is some advice."

"It's like I told you." Lucas nudged my shoulder, "Look at how much you're bringing home in a month. You don't want to spend more than half of your monthly income on rent." He paused. "Just make sure you're not living in a bad area either."

"If it weren't for the distance, she could live with you," Noah offered like he hadn't heard me talking about wanting to get out on my own. "It would give her a chance to keep an eye on her mom, even if they aren't talking." He tapped on the table as his attention went to a ball game on the screen. "Out of the four of us, you've been roughing it the longest. You might rub off on her. I mean in the right way." He pulled a face as he gave us a look. "Not the kind of preferred rubbing off."

"That's where you two need to get your damn minds out of the gutter." Lucas rolled his eyes. "Even if Frankie were to move in with any of us, it wouldn't be sex all the time."

"Thank you." I cupped my face in my hands. "I work, I come home and crash. Living with Sara, I spent the majority of my free time out with you guys or lounging in my room. Hardly think that would change."

"The difference would be you'd be out on the couch while we watched football or a movie," Lucas said evenly. Then he made a face. "If she moved in with me, I'd put her to work painting walls."

"I'm not thinking about sex with her all the time." Bryce slurred a little before he seemed to realize he was a little too drunk. He shoved his shot into the center of the table. "I'm just kind of hard up and now I'm drunk, so shit's not gonna work right."

"Disappointing, you promised me sex in exchange for helping me move," I mocked lightly.

"If it weren't for the fact I knew you were fucking with me, I'd get some coffee." B glowered at me. "Then I'd give it to you."

Noah picked up the shot glass and kicked it back. He made a noise and thunked the glass on the tabletop. "I think you should move in with Lucas. Buy a car. That'll piss your mom off. A sports car, some shit a hot shot doctor would drive."

"That explains that shit you drive." Lucas chuckled. "I heard your mom bitching about that when you first showed up with it from down the street. I stepped outside to see if I'd get a good view of her kicking your ass."

"She was kind enough to kick my ass in the house and not out in the yard," Noah said snidely.

I had my phone out as they went back and forth. I had my bank app open, and I was looking at the direct deposits into my savings. "A car would run me what? Three to four hundred dollars a month?" I glanced at Lucas. "How much would you charge me in rent?"

"More if you get luxury. I highly suggest it. I'd go BMW or Audi. They both pull off sporty and luxury enough to make your mom pull out that 'I brought you into this world, I can take you out of it' threat," Noah offered with a grin. "If you go that route, you're probably looking at anywhere between six and eight fifty a month."

"The spare rooms are kind of small. The house was built back in the eighties, and I didn't make any attempt to add more closet space. We could do three hundred plus splitting the utilities. That might be about four hundred total," Lucas offered, and I felt him get closer. I offered him a look at my phone, so he got to see what I was working with.

"How much rent do you pay a month, B?" I didn't look up when I asked it, but I was just trying to do the mental math.

"Pretty sure I'm at eight fifty plus the extra shit," he slurred. "That's a studio, too. The building is marketed as high end, but the walls are all like fuckin' paper. I hear my neighbors, and my neighbors hear me. S'why I never bring you home. I'd love to though."

"I'm at twelve hundred," Noah offered. "It's one bedroom, but you've seen it. Plus, there's a little bit more insulation in the walls, so my neighbors aren't as privy to what's going on in my apartment." He made a noise. "Once you get started, you'll be making more money. But you gotta build up to that, don't you? I mean I realize you got some money saved up while she was paying your bills, but that'll go fast if you go for a high-end apartment."

"This was something I was hoping I could hold off on searching for," I grumbled. "But it's my fault for not wanting to fully leave the nest. All of this..." I sighed a little as I sat back in my seat. "It's all my fault."

"I told you we could go back," Lucas offered. "I'm sure if she knew that you ended it, she would overlook it."

"No," Bryce whined. "No going backward."

Lucas drew closer and turned my phone in his direction. "There's enough to put a decent down payment on a new car. Or we can go used and probably have the majority of it paid off. If you want to live in a half-finished house. I haven't even started working on the kitchen."

"Fuckin' put us to work then," Bryce offered up. "We got less to worry about if she moves in with you than we do if she gets her own place." His face was a little red from his drinking, and he was heavily leaning forward. "You got this bad habit of picking up losers when you're away from us. I don't need you getting distracted by another dude who's gonna poach time away from us." He hit the tabletop. "I've had enough of that shit. Move in with Lucas."

"Calm down." Noah patted the other man on the shoulder. "Pretty sure you ain't gotta worry about other men anymore."

"I'm gonna remember he offered to help do manual labor," Lucas snorted. "Don't try to lawyer him out of it because he's drunk."

Noah pfted and waved a hand. "He's not the only one. This is supposed to be a night out. We're all supposed to be having fun."

"I'm just using you guys as sounding boards while I have a breakdown over this dilemma of mine," I snarked at the two of them. "Getting this adulting shit down isn't something I was ready to do. Sorry it's not entertaining you."

"Use me as a stepping-off point then." Lucas rolled his eyes. "Get a car so you can drive to work, and once you get that paid off, you can move on to something bigger."

He paused then, like he was considering something. "Paying off a car might be a little too long. Let's start for six months or a year. If it takes you five years to figure out bills and shit, you might want to move back in with your mom."

"Damn," I sighed. "Don't pull punches, man." I closed my phone and took in the three men around me, all of whom had been out of school and out on their own for longer than I had. "Fine. I'll use Lucas as a stepping-off point as long as I'm getting my own space."

"Good. I'll give you the benefit of picking the color of paint you're going to put on the walls." He stood. "I gotta piss. But if we got it figured out, then we can get you out of that apartment. One less thing you have to worry about." He patted my shoulder and left me with Bryce and Noah.

"So you'll be out from under your mom's wing and right under his." Bryce grunted and got up, too. "He's not gonna smother you like your mom did at least." He wavered and held onto the back of his chair. "I can't wait to get all this shit settled and get us back to normal."

18

I didn't wait for the end of the month to start packing. Since I lived mostly in scrubs, I didn't feel bad about packing my clothes away in boxes. At some point, I'd made it to the hardware store with Lucas to pick a color for my room. There was something to having a say to what the look of my space would have.

I never got that in Mama's house. I didn't have posters on the walls or the chance to paint them my favorite colors. The bedding was what Mama gave me, often muted and neutral, or flowered and way too girly for me. Something that carried over even when I moved out. It had been such a habit of having neutral colors, I didn't consider upgrading my comforter to something I would've liked.

But covering the primed sheetrock in a pale blue was more satisfying than anything I'd done since I moved out of Mama's house. When Lucas wanted to carry the color down the hallway, I was eager to help him paint. I understood why he had pulled the house down to the bare studs now. If just painting the halls gave me a certain feeling of creating something, what was the feeling he got while he was putting the house back together?

I didn't ask. The house and the project that it became started after his mother's funeral, and even after all these years, this was the closest he'd ever gotten to finishing it. I knew there'd been good memories in the house for him, but the bad probably outweighed the good. Watching his mother struggle, going without a father that didn't seem to give a damn, stripping down the house like he had would give him the opportunity to put good memories into it.

"Are you ever going to finish your house?" It was something we would ask at any gathering that fell back to his place, something that wasn't often before we moved to the next step.

"I work my ass off and hardly have the time." He rolled a shoulder like it wasn't a big deal. "Besides, everyone needs a project to keep themselves out of trouble."

While Bryce, Noah, and I all had classes to attend to, Lucas had his project and work. It was something I knew having been his friend, but it was the first time I'd gotten a real glimpse of him working. It was just painting, not strenuous, but there was a quiet about him that came with him rolling the paint onto the wall. Focus that I could appreciate.

"I like this color," he murmured as he got to the end of the hall. "Maybe we should go with something similar in the living room." He stopped as he turned into the empty great room. "Maybe a little darker, I don't know." He made a noise. "Having you here might make me finally finish."

I smiled as I finished the trim. "If you wanted it finished sooner, you would've. You could've had B move in to help," I said as I set the brush on the can I'd been painting from. "I know you probably have a better work ethic than he does."

"How long did he play football? High school and college?" Lucas snorted as he picked up my brush and walked into the open, unfinished kitchen. "If coaches couldn't whip his ass into shape for something other than ball, then I doubt I'd be able to." He took the brushes to the plastic tub that had been serving for a sink for I don't know how long. "I'm gonna get to work on the kitchen before you move in. I'm hoping to have the cabinets in, and I'll get a stove."

"You don't expect me to cook for you, do you?" I shot him a look. "Because you're in for a massive mistake if you do."

He let out a laugh then. "I'll do the cooking if you clean up after me."

"I might take you up on that." I smiled. This conversation had me thinking that this might actually work out. We had talked on the terms of it being a short period of time, but this had me thinking I could live with Lucas without a problem.

Perhaps Mama cutting me off would do the opposite of what she expected.

Between work and packing, I managed to find a car, too. I had Lucas' frank opinion with me and Noah to make sure I didn't get swindled on the car or insurance. While I might have been on my own, I wasn't. I had so many people watching my back, I felt better about it than I had the right to.

Was I ever alone in the beginning?

Mama had done a lot to raise me with her ideals, by her faith. But I fell from her sway by a lot, especially considering I was entertaining three men. I should regret disappointing her. I should be distraught that she hadn't made any attempt to reconnect with me. I should hate that she was ignoring my calls and hadn't bothered to return them no matter how many messages I left on her machine.

Yeah, Mama still had an answering machine.

When it came time to move in with Lucas, I had the help of all three of my boys. Even though I didn't have a lot of things, all three of them lugged boxes into the house. Lucas and Bryce were moving my dresser in when I noticed Mama in the yard. She must've been weeding the bushes from the front flower bed. I had a box of clothes in hand, and I stood there, waiting for her to turn to look.

They hauled my mattress out of the back of Lucas' truck, Noah toting the headboard. They didn't notice me. They were too busy working to settle me in a place they thought I was safe. Just like Mama was too busy pulling weeds to notice me.

But I still watched her.

I prayed and hoped she would turn back to me, that she would be the mother I needed. Because even after everything, even me doing what I needed to do to grow up, I still inexplicably needed her. Something told me I would always need her. It only mattered if she was willing to still be there.

A hand touched my shoulder. I didn't jump, but I didn't look away from Mama. I didn't want to miss it if she looked up to see me.

"We got the truck unloaded," Noah said gently. "Waiting on you to set it up."

She didn't look. She didn't turn once. Standing here this long, she had to have felt me staring.

Don't cry, don't cry, don't cry.

It wasn't the first time I had the mantra, and it probably wouldn't be the last time. I turned to go into the house with no more prompting.

19

It didn't take long for me to get settled. Lucas kept an easy-to-follow schedule. He got up before dawn and got home just after dusk. He was quiet, and it was like living with a shadow. Though I only ever saw him after I trudged in the door after a long shift. True to his word, he cooked, though it was mostly by microwave, on dishes that went in the trash, so I didn't have anything to clean up.

I adjusted to the commute and having to get up earlier. I knew how to drive a car; Mama had let me get my license. She just didn't let me drive outside of helping her do errands. The compact car I drove gave me a little wiggle room compared to Mama's large sedan.

The only problem I had so far was needing the reminders to pay bills. Every time a notification came up on my phone, I felt like an idiot simply for needing it. I was still a child playing at being an adult. I could do the work, but I needed someone to hold my hand and remind me to pay the bills. I never considered myself absentminded until now.

Fortunately, I knew the landlord, and he didn't begrudge me when I was late handing him rent and my share of the utilities. He just shrugged at me, while seated in a folding chair with his focus on the television.

"Rent usually is due on the first of the month. Sometimes you can negotiate a later date with individuals that own the property you live in. If they're cool about it. But when it comes to companies that own an apartment building, they're going to tack on a late fee every time you're late." He gave me a look. "Banks are the same way when you buy a house. If you're late paying the mortgage, then they're going to tack on a fee."

"I thought the house was paid off when your mother died." I bit my lip when I asked.

"Almost." He didn't look at me as he said it; his attention was on the ball game on the television. "There was just a few years left before the house was paid off. She worked her ass off and got the majority of it done by herself." He waited for a moment before he kept going, "Mr. Kemp made sure I knew how to pay bills on time after that. It wasn't shit I had to figure out the hard way."

"He didn't try to reach out to you after?" It wasn't something we talked about. His dad.

"He can fuck off. I don't give a shit about him, and I'm pretty sure the feeling is mutual. He's never paid child support. We're lucky Mom got him to sign the papers after the last time he was arrested," he murmured, not looking at me. "What about you? Have you tried to talk to yours?"

I shook my head and gave the television my attention, though I never cared for sports. I went to B's games, but none of that mattered now that he stopped playing. "I doubt they talk. Though I'm sure she blames him for this." I quieted. I didn't know how he would react. Knowing Lucas, he probably assumed it. "He hasn't reached out to me since I graduated."

Lucas raised a can of beer towards me. "To absentee dads."

I knocked my bottle of water against his can. "To absentee dads."

"You haven't changed your mind about all of this?" he asked after a length. "After being with all three of us, you haven't gotten it out of your system?"

"You think this was some kind of phase? Like now that I've been with everybody, I'll be ready to settle down with one of you?" I asked in return and shifted in the plastic chair. "It's not. This wasn't a phase."

"So," he looked at me then, "you're picking us over your mom? The one family member you have left?"

"I think you're overlooking everyone who's accepted what we're doing. They're my family. You are my family," I said simply. "It's not a matter of me picking you over Mama." I turned to watch the TV. I watched as the man up at bat swung and missed. "Mama picked her ideals over me. I don't fit her view of what's right. And what's right, to her, is more important than I am."

"It's comforting to hear you say that," he murmured and got up. "The longer this goes on, the more damage it will do when you change your mind." He left the TV on but sauntered back to the bedroom, the can of beer still in his hand.

I stayed in front of the television, watching each pitch without registering what teams were playing one another. I got up after the batter hit a foul ball, and I followed Lucas back into his bedroom.

The room was dark, save for the faint light from the bathroom. I didn't see him until he stepped back into the dark bedroom. He threw his t-shirt on the floor before he took notice of me. He didn't say anything, didn't offer for me to come in.

But I still felt the weight of his gaze.

I tugged my scrub top up and over my head and dropped it on the floor in the doorway. "I've not changed my mind after this long," I said quietly. "I'm not going to later down the line either." I considered him for a beat before I reached back to release the clasps of my bra. I rolled my shoulders and let the simple white lace fall to the floor. "I don't want to go to bed alone," I started. "I've shown Bryce and Noah just how I feel about them."

"I was there." His voice was hoarse. "I remember it."

"I want to show you that I'm not going to change my mind," I said evenly, my nerves twisting. Bryce would easily take me up on the offer. Noah wouldn't turn me down either. Lucas was the only one who I knew would tell me no. He was the only one who had to be talked into this.

Would I have to talk him into this now?

"I don't want to be a distraction," he said in the same tone. "I know how you feel still. I won't be able to distract you from your mom breaking your heart."

"You wouldn't be a distraction," I argued. "You've never been a distraction."

"I can't think of a time when you weren't," he growled at me. "Growing up and now." He released a low groan. "C'mon." There was a hint of desperation in his voice now. It pulled me into his bedroom and relieved me of the hesitation I'd felt before.

I had my shoes off, and before I came to stand before him, I loosened the string to my scrub pants and shoved them down around my ankles. I stood before him in the modest lace panties that matched the bra I'd been wearing.

Maybe there was something to what he'd been saying. There wasn't anything romantic about stripping down in front of the person you wanted. The question was, did it matter to him? I couldn't see his eyes. I couldn't tell.

A hand cupped my cheek, and the calluses on his thumb brushed against my skin, making everything stand on end. I drifted closer, reaching out to touch him in hopes that I'd create a similar reaction in him. My fingers traced his collarbone, then I drifted up and over his shoulders, wrapping my arms around his neck. I pressed against him, and the feeling of the coarse hair of his chest against my breasts had the peaks tightening.

"It's not been just me and you," he murmured, close enough to kiss. "Since all this started, I've shared you with someone else."

"Not this time." I went in to kiss him, and he pulled back out of reach. "This is the first opportunity for it to be just me and you. This isn't a distraction." Since he wouldn't let me kiss his lips, I kissed his cheek, nuzzling the scruff until I found his throat. I felt him swallow and the growing hardness of his cock against me. "This is me making sure you know just how I feel."

"I know how you feel," He didn't bother to stop me. "I've felt it. I've heard you say it." He pulled away enough to press his brow to mine. "I know how you feel." He kissed me then.

I didn't have doubts about how Lucas felt. But in moments like this, the part where it wasn't obvious that he would let me have him, I doubted he would give in. He'd turned me down more than once before. He didn't seem to have any issues telling me no.

This time, as he deepened the kiss, I realized he wouldn't turn me away this time. His hand wound in my hair, and he tugged my head back, taking control like I hadn't. I felt the hunger he must've kept capped down for weeks.

An arm was around my waist, and he tugged me closer, then moved. I didn't get any sort of orientation as to where he was taking me until he pushed me away. I didn't get the chance to catch myself, so I fell backward with a shriek, only relaxing when I felt his bed at my back.

He stood over me, eyeing me in a way I hadn't seen since the night all of us had been in his bed. I clenched my thighs together, trying not to get caught up in memories and stay right where I was. I wanted this just as much as I wanted him. The look he gave me told me that he felt the same. His thumbs hooked my panties at the waist, and he tugged them down my thighs.

Lucas didn't bother with his own shorts. He just leaned over me to catch my lips in another kiss that had me aching for him. He cupped my face again, keeping me possessed by the feel of his lips and tongue. His hand skirted down from my cheek, following a line down my neck to caress my sternum. He stilled there, his fingers splaying out to tease the curves of my breasts.

He pulled away to give us both a breath. "These tits have caused so many problems from the moment they started to grow." His hand shifted, so he cupped me, and his thumb teased one tip. "We were all okay until you started to get so ridiculously beautiful."

"So, this is all my fault?" I managed to gasp.

He snorted out a laugh against my lips. "It was your idea. You claimed responsibility for it all." He brushed his scruffy cheek against mine, making me shiver. "Are you going to argue with me because I'm giving you all the credit?"

"I did," I murmured, inhaling deeply when he followed the path his hand had taken. "It was my idea, but B started it."

"Did he?" His teeth scraped against my skin, and I arched my back, hoping he would take the hint.

"He put the idea in my head," I admitted just as he pressed his face between my breasts. I dug my fingers into his hair, and I held onto him as he bit lightly at the sensitive skin there. He latched onto the skin, suckling on it so it pulled something between my thighs.

He'd been hovering over me, then I felt the weight of him as he seemed to get drawn in by either the touch or the taste of me. Or maybe it was the noise I made. I didn't realize I was making noise until I heard it bounce back off the bare walls of his room. Everything seemed to echo, from the noise I made to every groan and growl that came out of him. The noises he made, even with me just scraping my fingers through his hair and along his shoulders, affected me just as much as his mouth and tongue did. It made me oh so conscious about how much I needed this. How much I needed him.

"Please." It came out of me with a breath. At this point, all I could think of was having the connection. Reestablishing it as I had with Noah and Bryce. So there wouldn't be any doubts. So that Lucas would know that I loved him, too.

"There's no rush," he whispered against my skin. "No one else here but me and you. No rush."

I arched up in irritation, trying and failing to get him to have a higher sense of urgency. He pressed his hips down against me, settling between them. I wrapped my legs around his waist in the event he decided he would try to draw this out further by pulling away.

It didn't seem to bother him; he still had his shorts on. He kept teasing my breasts like he would be content to just stay there, as if we both hadn't worked all day. I whined and pressed my hips against his stomach, grinding against him with some sort of relief. He had stoked me to the point of impatience, and he didn't seem to be inclined to do anything about it.

"Damnit, Lucas," I hissed.

"What?" he asked around my skin. "Not enjoying yourself?"

I shifted my legs from around him and shoved him back until I was on top of him. He didn't struggle, but he kept me close, smirking at me from where he was positioned against my chest.

"It's not a matter of me not enjoying myself, you just have to draw this out to the point that I'm gonna want to pull out my hair. Or yours." I knotted a hand into his hair and gave it a tug for emphasis. "Maybe it's better if I show you what I'm talking about."

I slid down to the floor before he could protest. With the lack of a bed frame, it didn't give me far to go. I tugged his shorts down with me, frustration showing when

I didn't gently tug at his boxers along the way. He propped himself up on his elbows, the look in his blue eyes undeniable lust.

"You keep saying you want to show me stuff, Frankie. So far, all I see is impatience." He tsked at me.

"I never took you as a tease, Lucas." I found a bravado and boldness that had me taking up his half-erect cock with a surety I normally wouldn't have. "I can only imagine how you'd complain if I teased you."

"You don't hear me complaining," he started to say with a bit of cockiness, only to have it end with a hiss as I stroked his length.

There was a temptation to just leave this as teasing touches. Give him an idea just how he made me feel. But if I was too impatient for his affection, I couldn't draw anything out to see him squirming. I pressed between his knees and decided to use my tongue to follow the motions of my hand.

As soon as my fist capped at the head of his cock, I followed to swallow it. The noise he made was better than any other sound I heard echoed off the bare walls. I looked up to see that I had his full attention. I hollowed my cheeks and followed down the line of his hardening length. His pupils dilated as he watched his cock disappear into my mouth.

It was thrilling to watch his reaction, to hear the long, drawn-out groan as my fist stopped at the base of him, and my lips met my fist. Could I go further down? I moved my hand, gripped his hips, and took him the rest of the way into me. I gagged and struggled to breathe for a beat before I pulled back up for air.

Lucas flopped back on the bed then, and I swooped down to swallow his cock again. I wasn't the most talented when it came to this. It always seemed like a chore, and I never thought much about what I was doing to the man I was going down on. But every noise Lucas made went right through me, making me clench my thighs together and squeeze for some sort of relief.

I adjusted everything I did to see just what would make him moan. Each time I swallowed his cock all the way, he made a pained noise that made me feel so powerful. I swirled my tongue around him and felt the buck of his hips against my mouth. I hadn't intended on teasing him, but here I was. I enjoyed every minute of it.

His hand dug into my hair, and he stilled me by pulling until all I could do was suck on him. I looked up to meet his glassy-eyed glare.

"Made your point," he gritted at me. "Now you can stop, or you can have me bust down your throat. Which is it gonna be?"

I considered it, breathing heavily through my nose as I eyed him. If I let him come now, there was a good chance I'd go to bed without, not that I didn't expect him to reciprocate. But I wanted him in me, not just in my mouth. I wanted his cock spreading me apart.

Slowly, I drifted up the length of his cock, enjoying every twitch he made and the hiss that came out of him. I didn't bother to shake the hand from my hair, but I did put both my hands to his shoulders and press him back on the bed. I crawled up onto him and straddled his hips with every intention of just sinking down on his length.

His hands on my hips were the only thing that stopped me. "Condom," he barked at me. "I think I got one in my wallet. I'm not gonna be stupid and say my pull-out game is strong after you were just sucking me off."

"Maybe I want it this way," I shot back.

"Despite what Mrs. Kemp and Mrs. Wilks said, I don't think they were talking about giving them a grandkid now, Frankie," he snapped at me. "You still got three years to go. You can't throw away all this hard work just because you feel like you've got to prove a point."

"I'm not trying to prove a point." I released a breath. "I'm on birth control. I've been on it for a few years now, Lucas."

"Pretty positive that shit ain't one hundred percent," he argued further. "Is that a risk you want to take?"

"Condoms aren't one hundred percent either." I reached down to position his cock at my entrance. I pressed down as much as he would allow so that at least he could feel the wetness that had gathered there. "They fail about three percent of the time, more if they're expired or stored incorrectly. Where do you keep your rubbers, Lucas? Your wallet?"

"I can't believe you're arguing with me about this." He looked like I might've won him over. Then his eyes narrowed. "Have you done this raw with them?"

I didn't need to ask for clarification. I just looked at him trying to decide if jealousy had him asking this or not. "Not yet." I decided to go for the truth. "Though I'm sure Noah or B wouldn't protest nearly as much."

"This," he gritted out as he let me sink down onto him. "This is a terrible idea." The protests seemed to die, and his eyes fluttered closed as I was fully seated on him. His breath caught, and he held me still with a little bit more desperation than his talk before. "Fuck!" The curse came out of him pained. "This was a bad idea."

There was definitely something to this, sex without a condom. When it came to the men in my life, I could trust them to be clean; I knew everything about them. I wasn't worried about catching something; the only risk was getting pregnant. Right now, that wasn't a major worry.

"I'll get the morning-after pill tomorrow," I assured him. I wouldn't stop now. "Next time, I'll make sure we have spermicide. I'm already on the pill, and I'll see if it's practical to get an IUD, too." It wasn't, and I might've just been saying anything to appease him. I moved despite the firm grip he had on my hips. I rolled on him, feeling every delicious inch of him as he moved into me. "Fuck," I whined. "Might need to swear off condoms after this."

It wasn't just a matter of how good it felt. There was also the dark look he managed to give me. Up to this point, he'd just let me ride him. He held onto me to keep me from shifting too far back and ending up in the floor. But the longer I rolled on his hard cock barrier free, the more he twitched under me.

Try as hard as he wanted, there was nothing left for Lucas to do but give in. He released a groan that rocked through me as I rocked on him. Then he sat up. His arms were around me, giving me a bit more stability and bravery to lean back to angle for a deeper thrust.

"Terrible fuckin' idea," he gritted at me as his hips moved to meet mine. "You're gonna end up pregnant. What the fuck are you going to do then? Prove your mother right?"

"If it happens, it happens." I propped myself up with my hands on his knees. "I've lived with someone else's plan for me in mind. Now I'm finally doing what I want." His eyes opened and connected with mine. "It feels too good and too right to go backward now, doesn't it?"

"What're you gonna do when I say I can't fuck you with one anymore?" He tugged me closer as he asked. "What're you gonna do when you spoil me and them with this?" Then he stood, putting me off balance and making me cling to him for fear of falling. I clenched around him tightly, and he released a string of curses that would've gotten him grounded for months when we were kids.

As soon as my back hit the mattress, I relaxed. I should've known he wouldn't drop me. I kept my arms around his shoulders and my legs around his hips. Since he was taking control, I didn't want to give him the opportunity to think he could tease me as he had before.

It didn't seem to be something he intended. He found purchase with his feet on the floor, and he thrust into me with a bit more gusto. It made the short ride I'd given him moments ago seem uncoordinated. I just clung to him, letting the feel of him in me heighten the grind of his hips against mine.

Our breaths mingled. Every noise he made in my ear went straight through me. I buried my face against his throat and moaned his name.

"I didn't want to rush this," he hissed, and then I felt a hand press between us. His fingers desperately flicked over my clit, pushing me further along until his name became a plea.

"I love you," I choked out against his skin.

Another string of curses came out of him, and I felt him explode. His hips kept up a stuttering rhythm even as his cock twitched within me. He kept me pinned under him, the hand between us still working until I arched up against him. He worked me through the orgasm until I melted beneath him.

We stayed connected with him breathing heavily on me. His weight wasn't overbearing; it was just as comforting as the rest of him. This should've worn me out. My muscles were definitely twitching from the excursion, but I didn't feel the normal pull of exhaustion. Just the satisfying hum of nerves reconnecting from where he'd blown them apart.

"S'terrible idea," he murmured, sounding drunk.

"Which?" I traced my fingers down his back. "Sex without protection or the fact I said I love you?" I tried to sound nonchalant about it, but it was a failed attempt. My voice quaked, and for some odd reason, I was afraid. There'd only been one other time I'd been afraid of Lucas, and it was at the beginning of all this.

He propped himself up on his elbows, and I could see the sleepy satisfaction in his eyes. His eyes were half-lidded, and I knew that I would like nothing more than to see this expression on his face more often. His hands came up to cup my face, keeping me in place when he found a way to cut through the post-sex brain to give me an intense look.

"I do love you." His voice was low, and with the lack of space between us, there was no way to hide what his words did to me. "There's nothing about loving you that is a terrible idea." He gave me a light kiss, a careful brush of his lips against mine that still managed to seize my heart.

Since I'd moved in, there hadn't been any moments of affection between the two of us. He was firm on the stance of being a friend and roommate, something I hadn't known how to take. This, though, was something I enjoyed.

"None of this seems like a terrible idea to me," I breathed against his lips. "Except for maybe the fact you've kept me from being able to coerce you into doing this sooner."

"Too much of this will make me want it on a regular basis." He looked like he was considering something, then I felt it as he pulled out of me. I whimpered at the loss, but the connection between us still felt solid. "Just like going raw is a bad idea," he grunted. "I'm gonna want more of that. That'll be too much of a risk, especially considering you'll have to do it with Noah and Bryce, too."

"You're going to make a big deal about it every time I want skin-to-skin contact, aren't you?" I asked without irritation. "Am I going to have to listen to you lecture about risks every time I try to get fresh with you?"

"Priorities, Frankie," he grumbled and rolled off me. He tugged the blanket and sheets back, then turned to look at me. "If you don't want me to lecture you, then let's not do this again."

"What?" I sat up. "So, we're not gonna have sex again?"

He took my hand and pulled me up to my feet. "Oh no," he sounded amused as he said it. "We're gonna have sex again. Priorities. So, we're both gonna have to suffer with me wrapping it up from here on out." He eyed me, I think to take in my nakedness with something that looked like lust on his face.

"Well, as long as sex is still on the table." I smirked a little and decided to let him tuck me into his bed. "Are you gonna do this every time?"

"Maybe," he snorted before sliding into the bed next to me. His arms came around me, and I immediately regretted ribbing him for it. "It's a hazard of a slumber party. Remember that the next time we all get together over here."

"I think that's something I can agree to." I settled against him. "Especially if we're gonna cuddle every time."

There was a snort of laughter as I settled against his chest. "Priorities."

20

Six months, it'd been six months since we started the arrangement where I was with all three of them. Our relationship hadn't altered too much. The banter was the same, and we still met at a bar or restaurant for a chance to rehash what was going on. It was a routine I had liked for so long, I was happy when no one said anything about dropping it.

The only difference was that they usually ended in sex. There were only a few occasions where I ended up with less than two of them. It was an adjustment I enjoyed figuring out. It made me hunger for each time there would be all four of us. I wanted to test just how much I could take between two men so I didn't have to worry about tiring out between the three of them.

My boys made a point of taking up any free time I happened to come across. With work, I was constantly busy, and there was little time to think about other things.

That was... until I had a day off. Lucas was busy, so much busier than I ever realized he was. He had his push mower out, and he made quick work from his place—our place—all the way to Mama's house across the street. When I stepped out onto the freshly cut lawn, he was making the rounds with a weedwhacker. He had the shirt he'd started out wearing off and over a shoulder. As he worked on keeping a straight line at the sidewalk, I noticed Mama in her yard.

Despite everything, she still had him doing the yardwork for her. Save for the perennials it looked like she was putting in under the front window. She had a large sun hat on and hadn't even bothered to give the man that had been cutting her grass a second glance.

Mama was still giving me the cold shoulder. She hadn't answered or returned any of my calls. Anytime I caught her outside, I didn't get a look either.

Something about seeing her there had me walking across the street barefoot. I was behind her before it even occurred to me what to say. The only inclination she showed that she was aware of my presence was thanks to that oversized hat. Otherwise, she didn't say a word. There wasn't even a shift outside of her carefully pulling the vivid blue larkspur from the plastic container. She liked blue flowers, and as soon as it was warm enough to plant, she would be out gardening.

"I'm happy," I said as I watched her shift soil out of her way with a trowel. "Well," I looked down at my toes, "as close to happy as I can be." I wrapped my fingers around the back of my neck, trying my best to calm my nerves even when I knew she probably wasn't listening. "I've gotten into neurology, and it's not nearly as stressful as the first four months of residency was. I'm well on my way to surviving the first year."

"Are you using this as a segue into telling me you're pregnant?" She didn't even turn to look at me when she asked the question. She just sounded snide as she judged me.

"Nope." I took a breath like I wasn't bothered by it. "Believe it or not, your yard guy is concerned about me not living my dreams. He's determined that I'll finish residency without getting pregnant." I waited for a beat to see if she would react at all. I didn't know what I wanted her to say. I just knew I couldn't go on with this. "If I were pregnant, would it make any difference? Would you still hate me? What about any baby I would have?"

She stilled. I wondered if she had even considered it. Probably not as much as Lucas had.

"You hate me so much for what I'm doing that you would turn away any grandchild you might have?" I demanded.

"Francine," she snapped like she knew I was loading more ammo into my verbal gun. She didn't turn to look at me, she didn't stand. She just kept digging into the dirt. "You will not guilt me into accepting what you are doing."

"It's a legitimate question, Mama." I shrugged. "Mrs. Kemp and Mrs. Wilks had the concern that there would be a question of who the father was, then decided that they loved all three of the boys, so it wouldn't matter." I decided I needed to see her face, so I moved so I could at least see her profile. "In your case, there's not a question of who the mother is. The only question is whether the maternal grandmother would give a damn. So. Would you?"

Mama stopped digging in the dirt, and her expression was hard to read at this angle. She didn't turn to me; she looked ahead at the already planted flowers. I wonder if she was even considering it.

"Of course their mothers would readily accept the situation you've created. They raised heathens and miscreants," she said snidely.

"The same heathen that cuts your lawn and does any work around the house you need?" I glanced up and saw Lucas walking towards us with the weedwhacker in hand. "Or is he a miscreant?"

"Francine," she snapped at me, finally looking up from the dirt. "What would you have me do? Turn away his willingness to help me." She stood and brushed off her knees. "Would you have me push a lawn mower around the yard? I could die from heat stroke or have a heart attack!"

"Is everything okay?" Lucas asked from the driveway. He looked between us warily before settling his gaze on me. The look I got said he was prepared to carry me back to the house.

"It's fine," Mama answered for me. "I'll need you to trim the hedges at the corner of the house too if you please," she instructed while still managing to look down her nose at him.

Lucas eyed me, but when I didn't say anything, he nodded and went to work edging and cleaning up along the flower beds where Mama wasn't working. It made it harder to talk to her, but as soon as he was far enough, I took advantage.

"Mama," I began again, "it's been long enough."

"I will not support you while you continue to do this," she shot back. "I will no longer pay your way to depravity."

"I don't want your money," I said, finding a way to keep my cool. "I don't want your approval. I just don't want you to shut me out or any baby I might have."

The roar of the weedwhacker was cut off, and I looked up in time to see the horror on Lucas' face. His mouth was wide open, and his eyes were huge. Obviously, he'd been eavesdropping.

"I'm not pregnant," I said to him so I wouldn't have him interrupting the conversation with my mother further. I looked back to her to see her eyeing Lucas with something speculative on her face. "But that's not the point." I heaved a sigh. "I don't want your money. I've needed to grow up since the moment I got out from under your roof. I'm growing up now, without your supervision, and I wouldn't change that for the world." I dragged my fingers through my hair and finally just let it drop. "All I want is for you to love me."

Mama's eyes widened, and that was the only reaction I could see. "I wouldn't turn away any grandchild you might have," she said after a length. "Even if I disagree with the choices you've made." She straightened and looked away from me before she rolled a shoulder and moved to the next plant that needed to be transplanted into the flower bed. "You are my daughter," she began haltingly. "I will always love you."

I relaxed, like every stress that had been sitting on my shoulders steadily let go. I didn't realize how much I needed to hear that. I wanted to hug her, but I didn't know how she would take it. "Does this mean you're going to start taking my calls?"

"Yes, yes," she said in a tone that suggested I was asking something ridiculous of her. "Now I would like to finish my gardening." She adjusted her gloves as she said it. "If you have anything else…" She started to lean down with the intent to get back to work, but she didn't get the chance to dismiss me.

I wrapped my arms around her middle as she went down. She released a loud 'oof' as she hit the grass. I had restrained myself enough, so I didn't knock her completely to the ground. I hugged her tightly, and I didn't realize how much I missed her until I realized she wouldn't want to see me. It was my fault, or partially. I had every opportunity to see her, to call her, and I never took it

"I'm sorry," I whispered into her hair.

There was a slight quiver that I wouldn't have noticed if I wasn't pressed against her. She patted my hand, offering me only a bit of comfort. "You aren't the only one who suffered here." Her voice was low. "And I'm sorry." I could feel the tension in her shoulders. "You're my daughter, I may not like what you do, but you will always be mine."

Epilogue

"I brought the beer," Bryce announced as he came out to the backyard. "That's what I was told to bring, so if you wanted anything more out of me, you're shit out of luck," he said as he pried open a cooler and stuck the six-pack he had under his arm into the ice. "Unless, of course," he grinned at me, "you want something sexy out of me."

"Food first," Lucas snorted as he turned a steak on the grill. "We should probably wait an hour after we eat, too." He didn't have an apron on or a chef's hat, something he'd earned the right to wear after the last few months of him manning the kitchen. I had the delight of learning that Lucas was a good cook. Seeing him in front of the grill definitely gave me some confidence that dinner would be delicious tonight.

"That's swimming," Bryce huffed as he popped open a can. "And you don't have a pool. But if you wanna start a fundraiser to install one, I'll make a donation." He took a pull of his beer, then paused as he considered it. He turned to look at me. "I reserve the right to use it when I want."

"That might as well be you asking to move in," Noah grunted from where he lounged in a folding chair on the porch. He was stretched out with his legs sticking out from under the porch's roof, so he could soak up sunlight.

"I mean…" Bryce paused and made for a nonchalant look as he surveyed Lucas' backyard. "He does have a free room."

"Are you asking?" I looked at him, then at Lucas to see how he reacted. "Didn't you just sign a new lease?"

"It was six months," B said defensively. "I got a few months left on it. There's nothing wrong with shopping around for a new place."

"Are you gonna wanna move in, too?" Lucas shot at Noah, keeping his attention on the grill. I couldn't tell if he was opposed to the idea. His shoulders looked stiff, but he wouldn't look at me. The bill of his ball cap shielded most of his face, making it hard to get a read on his expression.

"I don't want to live so close to my mom." Noah rubbed a hand at the back of his neck. "She saw me coming in and hollered at me that I still owed her grandchildren. I don't want her coaching us into getting Frankie knocked up."

"Ugh." Bryce moved to flop down in the chair next to Noah's. "Mom had been asking how marriage would work out between the four of us. Something about the legalities of us solidifying our relationship." He looked unsure as he fidgeted with his beer. "She'd only be able to marry one of us, right?"

Noah nodded. "It wouldn't be legal for her to marry all three of us. Probably be better off keeping things like they are."

"I don't want to get married," I spoke up so there wouldn't be an issue of it. I didn't want anyone getting any ideas about popping a question that I didn't want to answer. "It seems like it would only complicate things, and we've got things going so easily for us."

"What about insurance?" Bryce shot back at me. "What about kids?" His expression sobered as he spoke. "We have an agreement where this is just the four of us, but what if… what if things change?" I saw his fear on his face. "What if this is just the honeymoon phase?"

"It's not even been a year," Lucas objected. "We just got into a routine that fits all of us. Are you asking these questions because you're not happy with it?"

"No." B put his beer down on the concrete below him. "No. I'm happy. I gotta tell you, I never thought I'd have a chance with Frankie. Now that I've had her, I don't want to let go." He waved a hand at Noah. "You know what I'm talking about. The sex we've had with her has been some of the hottest sex I've ever had. You can see why I'd be paranoid about something good like this coming to an end, right?"

"Marriage is off the table." Noah sat forward, looking between the three of us. "Even if Frankie was up for that, it only could be to one of us" He shook his head. "Besides, marriage doesn't mean this would last forever. About twenty-four thousand couples get divorced daily."

"We don't have to get married," I interrupted the direction of the conversation. "And I wouldn't say that we're in a 'honeymoon period.' We just had a fight over where we would have this gathering," I pointed out. "I wanted to go to the bar. You wanted to go somewhere that had a bed readily available." I pointed at Bryce. "Completely ignoring the fact I'm on my period."

"At least you're not pregnant," Lucas grumbled as he picked up a platter to take our dinner off the grill.

"I dunno." Bryce stood to open the back door, so Lucas could step inside. "That shower he has in there is massive. We could probably fit in there and not have to worry about a mess." He waggled his eyebrows at me like he thought I might actually go for it.

"No, thanks." I got up to follow the steaks. They smelled too good to ignore. "Give me a few days, and we can talk." I went to the new fridge to pull out a bottle of water and the salad I'd put together earlier. It was my contribution to our dinner. I wasn't much of a cook, so salads were the best thing I could do.

"Kids on the other hand..." Noah began as he followed me in, "are something we should talk about." He paused at the island, probably my favorite feature to Lucas' kitchen. He tapped his fingers on the granite. "Are they completely off the table?"

I set the wooden bowl I had in my hands onto the table. I nervously picked up two spoons to give the lettuce and mixed vegetables an extra toss. "I-I don't know. I know what your mom said, and I don't want to make her angry. Just... just..." I swallowed hard as I struggled through my thoughts. I was surviving residency, I doubted I'd be able to do that with a kid in the mix.

"Not now," Lucas answered for me as he set the platter with the steaks onto the island. "Let her finish up residency and get what she needs to get done to be practicing before we can talk about kids seriously. That'll give us a few years to get the mechanics to a group relationship down. Then if it happens..." He rolled a shoulder, then moved to the microwave to fish out the potatoes. "Then it happens. We can face it when it comes at us."

I felt relieved. "Worrying about it right now will only make things stressful when they don't need to be." I smiled. "I'll be more careful, so accidents are less likely to happen, and we don't have to worry about it."

"Good," Lucas said pointedly as he pulled plates from a cabinet. They were new, like nearly everything in the kitchen. He'd gotten a few things secondhand, the dishwasher and sink for example, but he managed to find things that fit in with the contemporary style of the rest of the house.

"So…" Bryce snatched a plate from Lucas and picked through the steaks until he found one he liked the looks of. "This means it's cool if I move in?"

"Sure." Lucas rolled his eyes. "As long as you pay rent and realize you're sleeping in your bed most of the time."

"I work a lot." I sat on a stool, waiting for the boys to serve themselves. "By the time I get home, he's usually already asleep or going to bed."

"Not to mention she's probably too exhausted for sex," Noah added as he decided to start with the salad that Bryce turned his nose up at. "I remember when I was studying for the bar, I didn't even have the thought process available for sex."

"Depends on the day," I admitted. "If it's a hard day, then no."

I hoped I didn't have to explain it. Working in a busy hospital was just like it sounded. I hadn't had the opportunity to tell a patient bad news and, so far, any life-threatening issue I'd faced had pulled through for the better. I hadn't had anyone die on me. Fear ate at my gut with every serious case I assisted on. It would happen; I wouldn't be that lucky to get through residency without it.

Bryce's lower lip poked out before he cut into his steak. "Just killing all my sex-filled fantasies," he grumbled around a mouthful.

"It's not all about sex." I poked him in his side, digging my finger into his ribs until he squirmed. "Right?" I resisted the urge to pinch him.

"Right," Bryce whined, swallowing the food in his mouth. "Everything is just more fun with it."

SCARLET LANTERN
Publishing

Other Titles by Alyssa Clark

The My Boys Duet
-= Reverse Harem Romances =-

My Boys
Still My Boys

Nadia's Boys
-= Reverse Harem Romances =-

Reunion
Austin
Gavin
Vaughn

Stand Alone Reverse Harem Romances

Common Areas

The Decadence Club Series
-= BDSM Romances =-

Restraint
Claimed
Safeword

Keep up with all my latest releases at
www.authoralyssaclark.com
www.scarletlanternpublishing.com/alyssaclark

Made in United States
Orlando, FL
08 March 2022

15554181R00143